Demmix, the captain thought.

Picard would contact the *Stargazer* with a com device he had hidden on his person. And before long, both he and Demmix would find themselves safely aboard the *Stargazer.*

Simplicity itself.

Or so the captain expected—until he was driven backward by a blinding white, shrieking burst of energy. Before he could even wonder what was happening, he slammed into something hard, rattling every bone in his head.

Then Picard felt a second impact and realized he had stopped moving. *The floor,* he thought, feeling its flat, reassuring presence beneath him. *I'm lying on the floor.*

It was only then that he opened his eyes and saw the vision of chaos that had flattened the landscape of the plaza. There were merchants and kiosks and food strewn everywhere, victims of the savage and unexpected blast.

"Him! He's the one who set off the bomb!"

Picard turned to see who had cried out—and, more important, to whom he was referring. To the captain's surprise, the long, accusatory finger was pointing in a most uncomfortable direction.

At Picard himself.

Other *Stargazer* Novels

The Valiant
Gauntlet
Progenitor
Three

Requiem
Reunion
First Virtue

STAR TREK®

STARGAZER
OBLIVION

Michael Jan Friedman

Based upon *Star Trek:*
The Next Generation®
created by Gene Roddenberry

POCKET BOOKS

New York London Toronto Sydney Singapore

An *Original* Publication of POCKET BOOKS

POCKET BOOKS, a division of Simon & Schuster, Inc.
1230 Avenue of the Americas, New York, NY 10020

This book is published by Pocket Books, a division of Simon & Schuster, Inc., under exclusive license from Paramount Pictures.

ISBN: 0-7434-4854-5

First Pocket Books printing September 2003

10 9 8 7 6 5 4 3 2 1

POCKET and colophon are registered trademarks of Simon & Schuster, Inc.

Manufactured in the United States of America

For information regarding special discounts for bulk purchases, please contact Simon & Schuster Special Sales at 1-800-456-6798 or business@simonandschuster.com

For the winter warriors
of Farpoint 2003

Acknowledgments

Oblivion is a state of forgetfulness, but it would be an injustice for me to forget those whose efforts helped make *Oblivion* a book. First there's Margaret Clark, my editor at Pocket Books, whose unerring eye kept me time and again from looking like a complete idiot ("First it's a phaser, then it's a disruptor . . . it can't be both, can it?"). Then there's Scott Shannon, my esteemed publisher and one of the most decent human beings on the planet. And finally, there's Paula Block, executive director, publishing at Viacom, to whom *Star Trek* book readers owe a greater debt than they know.

I would also like to acknowledge the contributions of actress Whoopi Goldberg (you may have heard of her) and actor Paul Dooley, along with the writing staffs of *Star Trek: The Next Generation* and *Star Trek: Deep Space Nine,* who created and developed two of the characters around whom this narrative revolves.

STARGAZER
OBLIVION

Chapter One

JEAN-LUC PICARD WAITED for the octagonal portal in front of him to iris open with a faint scrape of metal on stained metal. Then he stepped through the resulting aperture, leaving behind a heavily ribbed cavern of polished duranium that had once been the cargo bay of an Yridian freighter.

Had this been any other Yridian vessel, Picard would have been entering an airlock, the black, frigid vacuum of space visible through transparent slivers in the surface at its far end. Instead, he found himself in a short, unremarkable corridor, its only illumination the parallel tracks of tiny floor lights guiding his footsteps.

Several wildly echoing strides brought Picard to another octagonal portal. As before, he waited for the thing to blossom like a flat, metal flower. Then he emerged into the chiseled, black environs of a Tellati armory.

Of course, there weren't any weapons in this armory— not anymore. But Picard had seen enough Tellati hulks to recognize the rows of elaborately wrought clamps set at intervals in the bulkhead, designed to hold enough disruptor rifles for the needs of an entire Tellati crew.

Picard doubted that the armory's original owners would have approved of the bright, jazzy music currently wafting through it, or the airy, blue lighting, or the rich, buttery fragrance that teased the captain's nostrils.

But then, the armory was now serving as a bar of sorts—just as the cargo bay Picard had just left behind had been recast as the lobby of a rather seedy-looking spa.

In fact, if he kept walking through enclosure after enclosure and navigated correctly, he would find himself traversing bits and pieces of a great many vessels—not just Yridian and Tellati, but Klingon and Ubarrak and Orion, and on and on—a seemingly endless conglomeration of them.

Together they formed a strange and unique city—a city in orbit around a world that had never spawned life of its own. A city called Oblivion.

Or rather, that was the nickname it had been given by the earliest Terrans to frequent the place. In the original Ubarrak, it was called Obl'viaan.

Picard didn't know how or why the first two ships in the by now immense complex had been cobbled together, or who was responsible for the cobbling. As far as he could tell, no one else knew either.

But little by little, other ships had been added—derelicts and sections of derelicts, space stations and half-destroyed hulks of space stations, some old and some relatively new, some easily recognizable and some not. And gradually, the city called Oblivion had taken on a purpose.

It had become a place where merchants of all species and backgrounds could cluster—where they could peddle their wares and work out their deals without the specter of interstellar politics looming over them.

It didn't matter who was at war with whom, or who had offended whose leaders. In Oblivion, traders from both sides of the conflict could still carry out their transactions in peace. Nor did it matter whether they were selling medicines, high-yield plasma explosives, or the latest in exotic entertainments.

Nothing was forbidden. No peaceful commercial activity was off-limits.

But for all its license, Oblivion wasn't a lawless place. Quite the opposite. It had its government and its rules, and a contingent of security officers who were only too happy to enforce them.

Like the orbital city's merchants and traders, its security force was made up of many different species. And while those represented in the greatest numbers were Rythrian, Enolian, and Tyrheddan, there were also a few Vobilites, Dedderac, Lurassa, and even humans.

As Picard took in the confines of the armory, with its several humanoid denizens sitting along an obsidian bar or scattered among tables, he remarked yet again to himself how fertile Oblivion would be for scholarly inquiry.

It was especially true from an archaeological perspective—Picard's favorite since his days at the Academy. Where else could one find the aft section of a hundred-year-old Meskmaali squadron fighter? Or a Rigelian ore transport of a perhaps even earlier vintage?

Picard would have loved to have the time to explore the place, scratching his archaeological itch at each stop along the way. But since his arrival in Oblivion a couple of days earlier, he had been forced to devote himself to this one particular portion of the city—and his study of it had been anything but archaeological.

After all, he had a mission to carry out here.

And an unusual mission it was. Quite a change of pace from his normal duties, which called for him to direct the activities of an entire starship and her crew.

In Oblivion, Picard was only responsible for directing his own activities—and keeping his identity a secret in the process. He wasn't even wearing his cranberry-and-black Starfleet uniform, having exchanged it for a colorless set of civilian garments before leaving the *Stargazer*.

It was rare for a Starfleet captain to skulk around undercover, much less to do so entirely on his own. However, on this occasion he had no other option. When an opportunity of this magnitude came up, one had to seize the day.

If all went according to plan, Picard would be doing just that in a little more than an hour. But he didn't want to appear at his prearranged rendezvous point too soon, lest he attract undue attention.

He could have returned to his hotel, but it was a little too far away. Or he could simply have wandered about the place. But he preferred to remain there at the bar, which was only a short walk from his destination, and minimize the possibility of something going wrong.

Besides, no one would question the notion of someone sitting in a bar for half an hour. Even a short walk in the warm, dry environments of Oblivion was likely to make a fellow thirsty, and Picard was no exception.

Aiming to address the problem, he crossed the room and took one of the few empty seats in front of the bartender—a human-looking female, though appearances were often deceiving in a place like Oblivion. There were a number of species that looked human at a glance, but were something else entirely.

At the moment, the bartender was attending to a Tellarite—a corpulent, white-haired specimen—who was in the midst of what seemed to be a long-winded tale, if the eye-rolling of his fellow patrons was any indication.

"And then," the Tellarite said in that blustery tone characteristic of his species, "I told him to take his phase coils and get out of my sight. I'd been trading too long to lay out good credits for shoddy merchandise. 'Shoddy?' he bellowed. 'You wouldn't know a quality phase coil if it was inserted into your left nostril!' Naturally, I wasn't going to stand for that sort of abuse…"

Picard could see why the other patrons were rolling their eyes. Unless one was a dealer in phase coils, the Tellarite's saga was anything but riveting.

Nonetheless, the bartender didn't take her eyes off the Tellarite for even a second. She appeared to hang on his every word, no matter how uninteresting it might have been to anyone else in earshot.

And she wasn't just listening because she had to, it seemed to Picard. She was listening because she wanted to, because she actually *enjoyed* it.

Of course, it might just have been an act on her part, a tactic designed to help business. But if it was, it was a bloody convincing one.

The captain didn't even mind having to wait to place his order. He was content for the moment to watch the woman smile a serene and knowing smile at the Tellarite, and fill his mug with something viscous and ocher-colored.

The Tellarite seemed to appreciate it too, if his delighted snorts were an accurate measure. And his species wasn't known for getting along well with humans.

Picard admired anyone who turned in a good job, whether it was commanding a starship or maintaining a food replicator. And in his opinion, the bartender wasn't just doing a *good* job—she was doing a *great* one.

It would have been nice to have such a person doling out libations on the *Stargazer.* There was plenty of stress involved in running a starship; there were plenty of raw nerve endings at the end of the day. A bartender in the right setting would go a long way toward helping everyone unwind.

Unfortunately, it wasn't even remotely practical for the captain to try to shoehorn a bar into the *Stargazer*'s cramped, little lounge. And even if he could get one in there somehow, he doubted he could bend regulations enough to staff it with non-Starfleet personnel.

As he pondered the idea, the bartender began to move in his direction, appearing to glide the length of the slick, black surface. "What can I get you?" she asked, smiling at him as warmly as if they were old friends.

Very old friends.

In fact, Picard had to wonder for a moment if they had actually met somewhere before. But he ruled out the possibility in short order. He had been blessed with an impeccable memory when it came to faces, and the bartender's wasn't at all familiar to him.

Nonetheless, he found himself smiling back at her. "Tea," he said. "Earl Grey, if you've got it. Hot."

"Oh," she said, "I've *got* it all right."

Turning to the replicator mechanism on the wall behind her, she punched a code into its data pad. A soft yellow glow became visible through the device's transparent door. When it subsided, she opened the door and removed a steaming black cup.

Even before she placed it in front of the captain, he could smell the familiar, soothing aroma. Earl Grey, he thought with a rush of contentment.

"There you go," said the bartender. "You know, I don't get many requests for tea, Earl Grey or otherwise."

The captain grunted. "Really."

She tilted her head as if to get a better look at him. "Obviously, you're from Earth."

"I am," he said, "yes."

"But," she added appraisingly, "you don't miss it much. You'd much rather be out here, in the far reaches of space, where every moment brings the possibility of adventure."

It was true. Picard could have followed in the footsteps of his father, a distinguished vintner, but instead he had chosen to make a career for himself among the stars.

But was his thirst for exploration that obvious? So much so that a person he had barely met could sense it?

"Are you sure about that?" he asked.

The woman nodded confidently. "Pretty sure. When you meet as many people as I do, you develop a knack for knowing what makes them tick."

The captain wanted to speak with her further—on that or any other topic, well into the night if he'd had the time. Her manner was that pleasant, that inviting.

But he *didn't* have the time. He was on a mission. And pretty soon, it would call him away.

"Impressive," he told the bartender.

But he didn't continue to engage her. In fact, he made a point of looking around the place, as if he had some genuine interest in the furnishings. By the time he turned around again, the woman had moved down the bar to one of her other customers.

Obviously, she had taken his hint. Picard breathed a small sigh of relief—or was it disappointment?—until he realized that the patron next to him was staring at him.

Like the bartender, she appeared to be human—in her mid-to-late twenties, if Picard was any judge of such things. Her long, charcoal gray dress and elaborate hat of the same somber hue concealed what appeared to be an unremarkable build.

Still, the captain might have called her attractive if not for the unexpected look in her dark brown eyes. It was a desolate look. A look that spoke of loss and missed opportunities, of pain and humiliation.

Of surrender.

It struck Picard that she was the exact opposite of the woman who had served him his tea. This person seemed dead inside, hollowed out by some terrible ordeal, while the bartender couldn't have been more alive.

"Do I know you?" he finally asked the woman.

She stared at Picard a moment longer, as if caught in some strange kind of inertia. Then, in a voice as weary and defeated as her eyes, she said, "You've got hair."

It was a bizarre observation, to say the least. "Apparently so," he responded.

The woman's eyes narrowed. "You don't remember...?" Her voice fell like a wounded bird.

The captain looked at her. "Remember *what?*"

Her brow puckered. "No," she said with something like resignation. "Of course you don't."

Picard didn't want to leave it at that—not after she had fired up his curiosity. But his mission prevented him from pressing her for the information.

After all, if she *did* know him, she could expose him for who he was—and that would pretty much throw a hyperspanner in the works, wouldn't it? His best bet was to remain silent, and hope it was simply a case of mistaken identity.

The woman stared at him a moment longer, looking as if she was inclined to say something more to him. Then, with a deep and uncomfortably prolonged sigh, she shook her head and turned back to her drink.

And he turned back to his.

But as Picard sat there sipping his tea, he continued to watch his neighbor out of the corner of his eye—and every so often she would sneak a peek at him. Apparently, she still couldn't decide if he was who she *thought* he was.

Less than eager to give her a chance to do so, he finished his Earl Grey as quickly as he could. Then, plunking down the appropriate coinage as payment and gratuity, he left the bar and the woman in the hat behind him.

The captain hadn't intended to be on his way so quickly. He had hoped to nurse his tea for a while, to linger over it. Now he would have to proceed at an all-too-leisurely pace, perhaps even loiter here and there, lest he reach the location of his rendezvous too soon.

He frowned. In every plan, there was an x factor—an unexpected element. The woman in the unusual hat had been such an element.

He could only hope he wasn't going to have to deal with any others.

Chapter Two

GILAAD BEN ZOMA, the first officer of the Federation *Starship Stargazer* and her commander in the captain's absence, couldn't sleep worth a damn.

He had been lying in bed for hours—four, by his last count—and had succeeded thus far in making a detailed inspection of his ceiling, naming every crewman on the ship, and calculating escape velocities for a half-dozen different shuttle types from ten different Federation planets.

It wasn't the first time in his life that he had suffered from insomnia. The first time was when he was ten years old, and his younger brother Levi had come down with a bad case of Andronesian encephalitis.

Ben Zoma remembered catching a glimpse of his brother from the corridor outside Levi's bedroom. Levi had looked so small in his dark blue bedcovers, so pale, that it didn't seem possible he would survive another day.

Then their mother had shooed Ben Zoma away, lest he contract encephalitis as well. But he had seen enough of Levi to keep him blubbering under his blanket all night, afraid that his brother was going to die.

Fortunately, the disease wasn't as serious as Ben Zoma's imagination had made it out to be. Levi not only survived, he went on to run a Federation research colony on Bejarus III and have a couple of kids of his own.

Ben Zoma's brother was no longer a cause for concern. Jean-Luc Picard, however, was a different matter entirely. It wasn't that anyone expected the captain's mission on Oblivion to hit a snag. In fact, there was every reason to believe it would proceed exactly as planned.

But there were no guarantees. Hence, the first officer's inability to fall asleep.

With a sigh, Ben Zoma surrendered. Throwing his legs out of bed, he padded across the room on bare feet. Then he opened his closet, pulled on a clean uniform, and left his quarters.

There really wasn't any point in his visiting the bridge. Elizabeth Wu—the *Stargazer*'s petite second officer—was perfectly capable of completing her shift there without any inteference from her superior.

Nonetheless, by the time Ben Zoma reached a turbolift, he had already decided on the bridge as his destination.

He was waiting for the lift compartment to arrive when he heard the echo of distant footsteps. Glancing down the corridor to his left, he saw a crewman come into view from a perpendicular passageway.

The first officer recognized the man as Nikolas, one of the ensigns who had beamed aboard with Wu, just prior to their pursuit of the White Wolf. But as Ben Zoma recalled, Nikolas had been assigned to the day shift. There was no need for him to be up at this hour.

The ensign paused at the joining of the corridors and returned Ben Zoma's scrutiny. Then, like some kind of ghost, he picked up his pace again and was lost to sight.

Clearly, thought the first officer, a fellow insomniac. However, Ben Zoma had a reason to be up. He wondered if Nikolas could say the same.

He was still considering the question when the turbolift doors opened. Entering the compartment, he programmed in his destination. Then he watched the doors close, and felt the slight vibration that meant he was moving through the ship.

In this case, it was only a short trip. A few seconds later, Ben Zoma felt the vibration stop.

Then the lift doors opened and he stepped out, drawing glances from the officers on duty. They all looked surprised to see him, though no one commented on the fact.

Since Wu wasn't in the center seat, Ben Zoma guessed that she was in the captain's ready room. As it turned out, his guess was an accurate one.

Wu was sitting behind Picard's sleek black desk as Ben Zoma entered. "Couldn't sleep?" she asked.

He plunked himself down in the chair opposite Picard's. "Apparently not."

The second officer gestured to indicate the captain's desktop computer. "I was going over some more of those reports we received on the Ubarrak."

Ben Zoma chuckled drily. "Fascinating, aren't they?"

"Unquestionably," said Wu. "It's difficult to believe they used to eat their young."

The first officer grimaced. If he'd had trouble sleeping before, that image wasn't going to improve matters.

"I've heard," he said, "that they only practiced that sort of behavior during famines."

"Well," Wu responded without missing a beat, "I guess that makes all the difference."

Ben Zoma smiled to himself. "So what else have you learned about the Ubarrak?"

The second officer shrugged. "That they're crafty, belligerent, and capable of holding their breath for several minutes at a time. And that they despise the Federation and the Cardassian Union in equal measure."

"That's because we're in their way," said Ben Zoma. "They'd like to annex the entire sector."

"So would the Cardassians," Wu pointed out. "But neither of them can become King of the Hill as long as there's a balance of power here."

She was right, of course. As long as there were three political entities in this part of space, it would be hard for any one of them to grab any more territory.

And the Federation would be content if it stayed that way. However, its Starfleet strategists were of the belief that the Ubarrak were about to break the stalemate.

If the Cardassians didn't beat them to it.

Like the Ubarrak, the Cardassians were clever adversaries. But that was where the similarity between them ended.

The Cardassians were cold and aloof, a species that

preferred its own company to that of others. Unlike the Ubarrak's entry into the sector, the Cardassians' had been a slow and subtle one—the result of political alliances and trade agreements rather than conquests.

But it was a presence nonetheless. And there was no question at Starfleet Command that the Cardassians could and would strike militarily, if they believed the situation called for it.

"Which," the first officer said, "is why the captain's mission is so important to us."

The key to it was a wealthy, high-strung Zartani named Nuadra Demmix. A few years earlier, Demmix's wife and two young daughters were visiting a Zartani colony when it was set upon by an Ubarrak assault force.

According to the colonists' accounts, they didn't even put up a fight. In a matter of minutes, their world became a possession of the Ubarrak Primacy—but not before the assault force took the lives of twenty-four innocent Zartani, Demmix's wife and children among them.

Demmix was overwhelmed by a black tide of grief. As sometimes happens with members of his species in stressful situations, his metabolism shut down—so much so that he had to be placed on life-support devices.

It seemed like only a matter of time before he succumbed. But somehow, he hung on. And contrary to the expectations of his physicians, he recovered.

As Demmix insisted later, it was for only one reason that he came back from the dead: He wanted to pay the Ubarrak back for what they had done to him.

Before long, he came up with a way to do that. He would use his considerable fortune to find out more about the Ubarrak. After several months of paying off official after official, he wound up with key information on a new sort of tactical system being installed in the Ubarrak's warships.

By sharing that information with the Federation, Demmix would place the Ubarrak at a severe tactical disadvantage—one they wouldn't even know about until it was too late. It wouldn't bring back Demmix's family, but it would be a sweet revenge.

There was just one problem. The Ubarrak were reported to have designs on the Zartani homeworld, and it was their practice to hire spies in preparation for any major invasion.

With Demmix being a rather public figure, those spies could have gotten wind of his efforts. That meant that his plan—as well as life—was in grave danger.

So when he cut his deal with the Federation, he made sure that safe transport to a Federation world was part of it. In Ben Zoma's estimate, that was only fair. If Demmix was going to give the Federation a leg up on the Ubarrak, the least Starfleet could do was help him survive.

On his own, Demmix could obtain passage as far as Oblivion, or so he had indicated in his coded transmissions. However, the orbital city had its share of Ubarrak, and he was concerned that they would be looking for a Zartani headed in the direction of Federation territory.

That was where the *Stargazer* came in. And even more so, her captain.

Five years earlier, Picard had obtained a special shore leave to run an elite, long-distance race on a barren planet in the Elyrion system. One of the favorites in the field of nearly fifty competitors from more than twenty different worlds was a young Zartani named Nuadra Demmix.

As it turned out, neither Picard nor Demmix won the race, or even finished in the top five. However, they ended up parting as good friends. In the short time they lived and trained together, the Zartani had learned to like the human—and, more important, to trust him.

As if that weren't enough, Picard had gained a fair amount of experience with the Ubarrak in the course of his Starfleet career. He knew better than most of his colleagues how the Ubarrak acted and how they thought.

Under ordinary circumstances, Ben Zoma would have wanted to assume the risk of undercover work himself. After all, it was part of a first officer's job to keep his captain out of harm's way.

But in this case, Demmix had insisted on Picard. No one else would do. So if the Federation wished to go through with the deal, it would have to put the twenty-eight-year-old captain of the *Stargazer* on the line.

And all his officers could do was maintain a position outside the range of Oblivion's sensors, but within communications range of Picard—a frustrating place, to say the least.

"How long until we're scheduled to hear from him?" Ben Zoma asked.

"If all goes according to plan," said Wu, "less than an hour from now."

The first officer didn't feel quite so bad anymore about getting out of bed. He would have been called to the bridge in less than an hour anyway.

He looked at Wu. "You can go back to those reports, if you like. You won't even know I'm here."

She made a face. "I was almost done with them anyway. Care for some coffee?"

Ben Zoma smiled appreciatively. "I thought you'd never ask. Light and sweet."

As Wu got up to go to the replicator, the first officer took a deep breath. Waiting was always easier when one didn't have to do it alone.

Besides, he added, he was probably worrying without cause. With a little luck, things would go as well for Picard as they had for his brother Levi.

Picard couldn't help squinting as he emerged from the dimly lit hatch of an Ubarrak cargo barge into a large, six-sided plaza full of people and exotic food kiosks.

Situated at the juncture of half a dozen ships and their respective hatches, Six Corners Plaza was reputed to be one of the few enclosures in Oblivion that hadn't originally served as part of something else.

Picard believed it. The plaza's lofty ceiling, which framed a densely starred section of the void in its transparent, triangle-shaped panes, didn't look capable of withstanding the stress of faster-than-light travel.

Fortunately, it didn't have to. No one would be pulling Oblivion out of orbit any time soon—not when it performed so valuable a function for so many right where it was.

Picard peered through the ranks of the merchants who mingled and eddied in the plaza like a confluence of wild, colorful rivers. But two stood out from the rest.

They were Ubarrak, powerful and broad-shouldered, their slitted yellow eyes set deep beneath dark, over-hanging brow ridges. They scanned the enclosure with tiny, animal-like jerks of their heads, as if they expected an attack at any moment.

Typical of the species, the captain mused. And a positive survival trait. Without it, no Ubarrak bloodline would have lasted very long.

There were also plenty of humans, Yridians, and Vobilites at hand, not to mention a clot of Tellarites, a couple of silver-skinned Rigelians, and a squarish, elderly-looking Ajanni in a stately black robe.

But not a single Zartani—which meant that the individual the captain was seeking hadn't arrived yet. It worried him. *After all,* he thought, *I am right on time. He should be here.*

Then again, the fellow might have decided to arrive a minute or so later than expected. That way, he could make sure he wasn't standing in the plaza too long, exposing himself to observation and discovery.

Picard understood the sentiment. Had their positions been reversed, he might have been tempted to err on the side of tardiness as well.

The captain was still entertaining the possibility when he caught sight of the one he was looking for. *There,* he told himself, *on the opposite side of the plaza*...emerging from the triangular, red hatch of a Lurassin scout ship...

The fellow was a Zartani, as tall and angular as any-one of that species, but leaner than most. His eyes were a shiny black, his skin the color of bronze, and his mane

19

of white hair was bound in braids that fell astride his sharply chiseled face.

Demmix, the captain thought.

He had been surgically altered, but not so much so that Picard wasn't able to recognize him. As he stood there, he saw the Zartani's eyes move in his direction—and lock on him with an expression of relief.

In keeping with their plan, Demmix began to walk across the plaza. When he reached the captain, they would depart together for a less crowded part of the station, exchanging meaningless pleasantries along the way.

Then Picard would contact the *Stargazer* with a com device he had hidden on his person. And before long, both he and the Zartani would find themselves safely aboard the *Constellation*-class starship, cruising at warp eight point five in the direction of Federation space.

Simplicity itself.

Or so the captain expected—until he was driven backward by a blinding white, shrieking burst of energy. Before he could even wonder what was happening, he slammed into something hard, rattling every bone in his head.

Then Picard felt a second impact and realized he had stopped moving. *The floor,* he thought, feeling its flat, reassuring presence beneath him. *I'm lying on the floor.*

It was only then that he opened his eyes and saw the vision of chaos that had flattened the landscape of the plaza. There were merchants and kiosks and food strewn everywhere, victims of the savage and unexpected blast.

For a moment, Picard feared they were all dead.

Then, as the shock wore off, he saw them begin to stir. And as they stirred, they began crying out.

Some moaned in pain. Some cursed. Some called for help, and others demanded retribution against those responsible for their injuries.

Contrary to Picard's first impression, everyone was still alive. But the majority of the merchants were hurt in one way or another, some of them rather seriously.

Remembering his mission, the captain darted a glance at the triangular hatch of the Lurassin ship. But Demmix wasn't standing in front of it anymore. He had fled the plaza like a startled deer, and there was no telling in which direction he had gone.

Picard's first impulse was to go after his old friend, to track him down. After all, the Zartani held the fate of a great many people in his hands. Then he saw a Tyrheddan female reaching out to him for assistance.

"Please," she said, her single eye round with fear amid the brown folds of her skin, "please help me..."

The captain's teeth ground together. He couldn't ignore the woman's plea. As much as he hated the idea, he would have to find Demmix later.

Dropping to the Tyrheddan's side, he took a quick inventory of the wounds he could see. None of them seemed serious. However, there was a dark, wet spot in the vicinity of her ribs that seemed to be growing before his eyes.

"Don't leave me," she told him, clutching at his arm in fear and desperation.

Picard placed his hand over hers, feeling the roughness of her alien skin. "I won't," he assured her.

Without medical instruments or expertise, there wasn't much he could do for her. But he remained at her side, her hand in his, until security arrived in its black-and-blue uniforms and began tending to the woman's injuries.

At that point, the captain began to consider his next move. He looked around the plaza and saw no sign of Demmix. But then, he hadn't expected to.

As Pug Joseph, the *Stargazer*'s acting security chief, would have said, that horse had already left the barn.

Like Picard, Demmix would have suspected the timing of the explosion, which took place almost exactly at the moment the two of them were scheduled to rendezvous. It seemed unlikely that it was a coincidence.

And Demmix had been skittish to begin with. He would be even more so now.

Picard would have loved to investigate the facts surrounding the explosion—who had set it, for instance, and for what arcane reason. But he didn't have the luxury of the time that analysis would require. He had to focus on finding Demmix and getting him safely aboard the *Stargazer.*

All other considerations would have to wait. With that in mind, Picard got up and headed for the hatch of the Lurassin ship, reckoning it was as good a starting point as any.

But he had barely taken a step when he heard a guttural voice crack like thunder over the plaza: "Him! He's the one who set off the bomb!"

Picard turned to see who had cried out—and, more important, to whom he was referring. What he saw was a tall, slope-shouldered Yridian, his tiny eyes ablaze with excitement in his long-eared, wrinkle-ridden face.

And to the captain's surprise, the Yridian's long, accusatory finger was pointing in a most uncomfortable direction.

At Picard himself.

"I beg your pardon?" he managed to retort—rather lamely, he was afraid.

But before he could finish, a couple of security officers—a ruddy, long-tusked Vobilite and a purple-skinned Cataxxan—converged on him with their weapons drawn. Picard thought about making a run for it, but the approach of two additional officers convinced him that he would never make it.

The Yridian's lower lip curled with disgust. "The stinking human probably thought he would get away with it. But I saw him. I saw *everything*."

"You've got the wrong man," Picard protested evenly. "I'm not the one responsible for what happened here."

"We'll see about that," the Vobilite rasped skeptically around his tusks.

The Cataxxan jerked his hairless head to indicate a direction. "The detention facility is this way. And don't try anything—my weapon's not set on stun."

The captain noticed the gathering crowd of onlookers and cursed under his breath. He had hoped to avoid drawing attention to himself. Now, through no fault of his own, he had done a lot more than just draw attention.

He had become an object of intense curiosity—the human suspected of setting off an explosive device in the middle of Six Corners Plaza.

With a quartet of directed-energy weapons trained on him, Picard had no choice but to proceed in the direction the Cataxxan had indicated. As he did so, he saw the expressions on the faces of the merchants on either side of him.

Hatred burned in their eyes, no matter the shape or color or number of them—hatred and a desire for retribution. Nor could the captain blame them. He wanted to know who had set off the explosion as much as they did.

Perhaps even more.

His jaw muscles working furiously, Picard allowed himself to be escorted through a hatch and into another airlock—his mission suddenly very much in jeopardy.

Chapter Three

"ANOTHER CUP?" Wu asked.

Ben Zoma, who—through an enormous act of self-control—was still sitting on the other side of the desk in the captain's ready room, shook his head. "No, thanks. Two's my limit." He picked up the white ceramic mug the second officer had given him and peered into it, swishing around its contents. "Besides, I didn't even finish this one."

"It's a good blend, though," said Wu.

"It is," Ben Zoma agreed. "No complaints."

"Glad you liked it," she told him.

They both fell silent. But it was clear that they didn't really have coffee on their minds.

From the time the second officer poured their first cups, she had studiously avoided the subject of Captain Picard. After all, Ben Zoma and the captain were more than colleagues—they were close friends—and Wu had seen no point in adding to her superior's anxiety.

At least, until now.

"I hate to say it," she began, "but it looks like—"

"The rendezvous was a flop," Ben Zoma said, sparing her the trouble. "It never came off."

"And the captain hasn't communicated with us," Wu reasonably concluded, "because he's attempting to improvise."

Her superior looked at her for a moment. Then he shook his head from side to side.

"No. If he could have contacted us, he would have. Something is stopping him."

Wu smiled. "You sound so certain."

Ben Zoma shrugged. "You work with someone day in and day out, you get to know him pretty well—what he would do, what he wouldn't do. If we haven't heard from the captain, it's because he's got his hands full."

"So what do we do?" the second officer asked.

"That's a good question," he said. "We can't just swoop in with the *Stargazer* and try to pull him out of there—not unless we want to alert the Cardassians, the Ubarrak, and everyone else in the sector that something's going on."

Wu couldn't argue with the man's logic. "We hold our present position, then?"

"For now," Ben Zoma told her.

She didn't ask how long "now" would last.

But even if the captain was in some difficulty, there was no one more clever or resourceful in Wu's estimate. Surely, Ben Zoma appreciated that as well, and would give his friend every opportunity to succeed on his own.

"A day," he said abruptly.

Wu looked at him. "I beg your pardon?"

"That's how long I'm giving him," said Ben Zoma, as if he had read her thoughts. "One day."

Picard gazed across his cramped, brightly illuminated cell at the individual who served as chief of security for this section of Oblivion.

His name, according to the other security personnel in the detention facility, was Steej. Like all Rythrians, he had a lean frame, generous flaps of skin for ears, and eyes that appeared eager to escape their sockets.

His uniform, like those of the city's other security officers, was black and blue, with what looked like an inverted fleur-de-lis emblazoned in silver on the left side of his chest. His rank was denoted by a series of three concentric silver ovals that sat on his right shoulder.

The security director consulted the padd in his hand. Then he looked up at Picard.

"Your name is Hill?" he asked in a surprisingly calm and melodious voice.

"Yes," said the captain. "Dixon Hill."

It was the name of the hero in a habit-forming series of twentieth-century pulp detective novels. Picard had felt confident when he assumed the identity that no one in Oblivion would have heard of it.

"Mister Hill," said Steej, "we have a problem here. An explosion. Casualties. Property damage. And though we've secured a suspect, we have no idea why he would do such a thing."

"Nor do I," Picard said.

The Rythrian tilted his head, as if to examine his subject from a different angle. "You claim innocence, then?"

The captain shrugged. "I was headed for the plaza to get a bite to eat when the explosion took place. I know as little about it as you do."

"Yet we have a witness who pointed you out. He says he saw you set off a bomb in the center of the plaza."

"He's lying," said Picard.

An unpleasant, high-pitched piping sound emerged from Steej's throat. "I doubt it, Mr. Hill. Ioro Tajat is no stranger to this place. He knows what I would do to him if I discovered he was purposely misleading me."

"Nonetheless," said Picard, "he's lying."

The skin around the Rythrian's eyes twitched almost imperceptibly. "And Ioro has reason to do this because...?"

Picard shook his head. "I don't know what his reasons are. I only know I didn't set off any bombs."

"I see," said Steej. He consulted his padd again. "You're here on business. A dealer in—"

"Duotronic relays," said the captain.

It was his cover story, one he had concocted days before he actually set foot in Oblivion. And thanks to his Starfleet training, he actually knew enough to pass as someone who traded in such equipment.

"You have the relays on your ship?" Steej inquired.

"I do," Picard confirmed. "But my ship is elsewhere at the moment, making a delivery."

Actually, it wasn't his ship at all, but an Ajanni trader the Federation happened to have in its possession. In fact, though it was hardly common knowledge, the Federation kept a great many non-aligned vessels on hand, never knowing when one of them might come in handy.

In Picard's case, the trader had been used to drop him off, nothing more. No doubt it was already back in whatever obscure shipyard it had been plucked from.

"A pity," the Rythrian said archly. "If your ship were docked here, it would have lent some credence to your story. As it is, you could be almost anyone." He tilted his head again. "Even an assassin."

"Which I am not."

"Or so you say."

Picard felt a pang of resentment. It was true that he wasn't what he purported to be. But how could anyone believe him capable of setting off a bomb?

"Look," he said, "you've got no real proof that I did anything wrong. Only the word of a single witness. For all we know, it was *he* who set off the bomb."

"True," the security director conceded. "But I know him. And I don't know you."

"But there's no *evidence*," Picard insisted.

"Which," said Steej, "is no doubt as the guilty party intended. But we'll find something. We always do. Until then you will be our guest." His eyes hardened. "And if we find out you're lying, Mr. Hill, you will wish you had never *heard* the name Oblivion."

The captain forced himself to keep his mouth shut. He couldn't let Steej's threats provoke him into saying something that might expose him.

Unfortunately, the security director seemed determined to find proof of the charges against him. And even if he couldn't, it might be months until he satisfied himself that Picard was innocent after all.

By then, Demmix would be gone—or worse. And the Federation would have lost the information the Zartani had offered them.

"No doubt," said Steej, with a fluttering of his nostrils, "we will have occasion to speak again."

With that, he got up and gestured to the lone officer outside Picard's cell—a one-eyed Tyrheddan, like the wounded female in the plaza. The electromagnetic barrier was deactivated long enough for the Rythrian to exit, then restored to its previous intensity.

Steej paused to impart some instructions to the Tyrheddan. Then, with a last glance at his prisoner, he withdrew from that part of the detention facility—leaving Picard to stew over his circumstances.

Clearly, the captain thought, *this Ioro Tajat is lying through his teeth, purposely trying to get me in trouble. But why? And for whose benefit?*

And what about the bomb? Was Ioro Tajat in on that as well? And if so, had he set it off specifically to frustrate Picard's mission here?

The captain hoped not. Because if Ioro Tajat knew what Picard was up to, it meant someone had received advance notice of his plans to rendezvous with the Zartani.

Who might that someone be? An associate of the Zartani? Or—Picard hated to even consider this possibility—someone on his own ship?

He shook his head. His crew was trustworthy, every last one of them. He refused to believe that any of his people could have betrayed him this way, regardless of whatever temptation might have been placed before them.

It had to be someone else.

But either way, the Zartani was in danger. His survival depended on his ability to keep his identity a secret, and it appeared that the secret was out.

As Picard faced that fact, he caught sight of someone entering his part of the detention facility—someone dressed not in the black and blue of the city's security force, but in a charcoal gray dress with a large and unusual hat.

It was the woman who had been sitting next to him at the bar.

He regarded her with suspicion. After all, it was quite a coincidence that her path had crossed his a second time, and in the space of little more than an hour.

Might she have had something to do with the bomb? the captain wondered. *Or my incarceration? Or both, perhaps?*

And why is she here now? he asked himself. *To offer some tidbit of false information that will further damn him as a criminal?*

He watched through the transparent barrier of his cell as the woman approached the Tyrheddan security officer. Leaning forward over the desk between them, she whispered something in the fellow's tiny, round ear.

The security officer laughed, making a sound like rocks scraping together. Then he whispered something back.

Wonderful, Picard thought. *They are old friends.* How else could they be conversing so easily?

He shook his head, only now recognizing the full extent of his naïveté. The woman in the hat, the bomb, his accuser...it had all been a trap, and he had walked right into it.

How foolish could he have been? How blind? Cursing himself, he forced himself to watch as the security officer and the woman continued their conversation.

With his loudest laugh yet, the Tyrheddan pressed a stud on his desk and opened a drawer. Then he bent over to get something out of it.

Picard frowned. Were they talking about *him?* Commenting, perhaps, on how easily he fell prey to their scheme?

He was still wondering when the woman picked up a heavy-looking stauette on the security officer's desk and slugged him over the head with it.

As the officer collapsed in an insensible heap, the woman grabbed the handle of his hand weapon and slipped it out of his belt holster. Then she headed for Picard's cell.

The captain entertained the possibility that she would use the weapon to kill him. He continued to suspect as much as she purposefully pressed the pad in the bulkhead that would deactivate his cell's energy barrier.

But no sooner had the energy wall fizzled away than the woman turned the pistol around and extended it to him. He looked at her for a moment, caught off guard.

Then, warily, he took it.

"Come on," she said, "let's go!"

Picard had a million questions elbowing each other in his head. However, he resisted the impulse to ask any of them. After all, they had to get out of the detention center before any of the other security people came around.

Leading the way to the diamond-shaped hatch that served as an entrance to that portion of the facility, he touched the bulkhead pad beside it. The hatch opened quickly and quietly, exposing a long, straight stretch of corridor.

"Not that I'm complaining," the captain said with a glance at his companion, "but what made you decide to risk your life for a perfect stranger?"

The woman's eyes seemed to lose their focus for a second. Then she said, "I'm a pretty good judge of character. I didn't believe you were responsible for that bomb."

Picard recalled the way she had spoken to him at the bar, as if she believed they had met before. Maybe that was why she was inclined to trust him—because she felt she knew him.

"Even so," he said, "it was quite a gesture."

The woman shrugged. "I was in a tough spot myself a while back, and someone went out on a limb for me. Let's just say I was returning the favor."

The captain absorbed the information. "Then, whoever helped you, I'm indebted to him—as well as to you."

She made a sound reminiscent of amusement. "I'll remember to thank him for you."

The hatch at the far end of the corridor was shaped like an arch. Another bulkhead pad opened it for them, revealing a compact, well-lit room that might once have served as a lounge or a mess hall.

But now it was full of equipment—workstations, sensor readouts, and a half-dozen wall-sized banks of security monitors, displaying more than a hundred key locations throughout Steej's section of Oblivion.

Fortunately, only two of the workstations were manned by security officers. And even more fortunately, neither of those officers looked up to see who had entered the room.

At least, at first. And by the time one of them did, Picard had taken aim at him.

With a squeeze of his phaser's trigger, he sent a seething red beam across the room. The officer, a human, was blasted out of his chair.

The other uniformed individual in the room, a black-and-white-striped Dedderac, whirled in his seat and drew his weapon. But Picard was too quick for him. With another squeeze of his trigger, he slammed the Dedderac into the massive bank of monitors behind him.

The captain hadn't seen either of the officers move to sound an alarm, but he couldn't be sure they hadn't done so. Taking his companion's hand, which was unexpectedly cold to the touch, he drew her through the maze of equipment.

Even though he hadn't noticed any other security officers in the room, he remained alert for an ambush. But none materialized. He and his savior reached the exit unmolested.

Opening the diamond-shaped hatch they found there, they emerged from the detention center into a long, hangarlike space—one that had the inverted fleur-de-lis of security rendered in silver on each of its bulkheads, and a half dozen exit hatches. The place was surprisingly empty except for a single uniformed figure, who was standing in the center of the enclosure and searching himself as if he had misplaced something.

As luck would have it, the figure was Steej.

It seemed to Picard that the Rythrian hadn't noticed him yet. That was the good news.

The bad was that Steej was a good sixty meters away, too far for Picard to trust his accuracy with an unfamiliar weapon. And if he missed, the Rythrian would be close enough to the exit on the far wall to escape—at which point he could clamp down on the captain and his benefactor with all the power at his disposal.

Gesturing for his companion to remain where she was, Picard started in Steej's direction. He moved as quietly as he could, hoping the scrape of his footgear on the hard metal surface wouldn't betray him.

Fifty-five meters, he thought. *Fifty. Forty-five…*

That was when Steej turned, moved to do so either by instinct or perception, and looked back over his shoulder. Still closing on him, the captain squeezed off a blast.

At first he thought it was going to hit its target. Then he saw it slice past the Rythrian and bury itself in the bulkhead behind him.

With a curse, Steej pulled out his weapon and fired back. But by then Picard had gone into a roll. He saw a blur of bloodred brilliance, but felt no impact—meaning his adversary had missed as well.

Capitalizing on the fact, Picard came out of his roll and unleashed another bolt. This time, he hit the Rythrian in the shoulder, spinning him about and sending his phaser flying from his hand.

Holding his shoulder, Steej tried to run. But Picard

pursued him, took careful aim, and knocked the security director off his feet with a well-placed beam.

Satisfied that Steej wouldn't be calling for help until someone found him and revived him, Picard looked to the woman in the hat. She was waiting by the entrance to the detention facility, as he had instructed her to do.

"Which way?" he asked, his voice echoing urgently throughout the enclosure.

Without a moment's hesitation, the woman pointed to one of the hatches on her left. "That way," she said.

Trusting that she knew what she was talking about, Picard followed her lead.

Chapter Four

ENSIGN ANDREAS NIKOLAS DIDN'T KNOW how long his friend Obal had been speaking to him before the fact finally registered in his brain.

"...an Ubarrak warship," the Binderian said grimly. Then he looked at Nikolas, obviously expecting a reaction.

The human looked across the mess-hall table at Obal. He could have pretended that he had been paying attention, but he didn't think he would be very convincing.

"Sorry," he said finally. "I guess I wasn't listening to that last part."

Obal heaved a heartfelt sigh. "I don't believe you were listening to the first part either, my friend. Or the middle part, for that matter."

Nikolas stared at the platter of food on the tray in front of him. He couldn't even remember what it was that he had ordered. All he knew was that it didn't appeal to him anymore, if indeed it ever had.

"Maybe not," he conceded.

"I was telling you what happened to the *Yeager*," said Obal, "and how she barely survived her encounter with the Ubarrak near Turion Prime."

"Right," said Nikolas, doing his best to work up some enthusiasm for his best friend's sake—and failing miserably.

Obal's eyes screwed up as if he were trying to look *into* the human instead of *at* him. "If you like, we can talk about something else."

Nikolas knew what his friend was trying to do—the same thing he had been trying to do for weeks now. But it hadn't worked in all that time, and there was no reason for Obal to believe it was going to work now.

Still, he wasn't going to stop. That much seemed clear. Obal could be pretty stubborn when he wanted to be, especially when it came to what he perceived as Nikolas's welfare.

"I can't think of anything I really want to talk about," Nikolas said, wincing at how bitter and self-centered he sounded. He glanced at his friend. "Sorry, but..." He shrugged.

"It's all right," said Obal. "I understand."

No, thought Nikolas, *you don't.*

How could he? Obal hadn't seen the woman he cared about vanish in a column of light, transported not just off the ship but to a completely different reality.

A reality he would have made his own, if she had let him. But she had come to Nikolas's universe on a mission, and she had refused to abandon it—no matter how sorely she might have been tempted to do so.

And now Nikolas would never see her again.

Obal leaned closer to him. "I know it is painful, my friend. But it does you no good to pine for Gerda Idun. You must put her behind you. You must move on."

Easy enough to say, Nikolas thought. *Impossible to do—at least for me.*

Gerda Idun had shown up unannounced on their transporter pad, the apparent victim of a transporter screwup. Nikolas hadn't seen it, but he had seen *her.*

She was a dead ringer for Gerda and Idun, the human twins who served at helm and navigation on the *Stargazer*'s bridge. And yet, she was so different from either one of them.

Gerda and Idun had been raised by Klingons, but that wasn't the case with Gerda Idun. As a result, she was easier to read and to get along with. And before he knew it, Nikolas had fallen in love with her.

Then it turned out that her arrival on the transporter pad hadn't been an accident after all. She had been dispatched to Nikolas's universe to abduct the *Stargazer*'s chief engineer, Phigus Simenon, in the hope of shoring up a rebel cause in Gerda Idun's universe.

Thanks to Nikolas and then Gerda, the abduction never came off. Gerda Idun was sent back to her comrades painfully empty-handed—but no more so than Nikolas, who lost the only woman he had ever loved.

Worse, Gerda and Idun still lived and worked on the *Stargazer.* Every time Nikolas ran into one of them, it reminded him of what might have been.

It stinks, he told himself. He had no appetite. He couldn't sleep. He couldn't even rest without thinking of Gerda Idun. And he didn't know how much more he could take of it.

"You need to be alert," said Obal, breaking into Nikolas's thoughts, "if you're to receive the promotion that the captain spoke of."

Picard *had* mentioned such a possibility. At the time, Nikolas had considered it the best thing that could possibly have happened to him.

Funny. He even remembered the words the captain had used—or most of them.

"I would take special care to avoid physical conflicts with your colleagues, whether they start in anger or not. It would be a shame to mar what is becoming a most compelling case for promotion."

But that was before Nikolas saw Gerda Idun disappear on that transporter pad. Now he didn't give a damn if he got a promotion or not. The whole thing was an abstraction, hardly worth thinking about.

Besides, he had disobeyed Picard's orders. He had gone to the transporter room when Gerda Idun was scheduled to leave, instead of reporting to his assignment in engineering.

The captain hadn't seen fit to take him to task for it, perhaps because Nikolas had fortuitously had a hand in thwarting Gerda Idun. Still, he doubted that the incident would count in his favor.

The ensign shook his head. "I don't think I'm hungry anymore," he told Obal. Then he got up, lifted his tray off the table, and started for the matter-recycling bin.

Too late, Nikolas saw a flash of scarlet uniform. Before he knew it, his meal—whatever it had been—was decorating the front of his tunic.

And a tall, broad-shouldered Bolian, who had been adorned with the steaming contents of his *own* tray, was standing there glowering at him with angry black eyes.

Nikolas knew the guy. His name was Hanta. He worked in the science section under Lieutenant Kastiigan.

Hanta was known for having something of a temper—a rare quality in a Bolian. To that point, Nikolas had never considered it a problem.

But it became one when Hanta uttered a curse in his native tongue and shoved Nikolas backward into another crewman, who was in turn knocked halfway off his chair.

Nikolas felt the hot rush of anger flood his face. He could have tried to quell it, subdue it—but he didn't want to. All he wanted to do was shove Hanta's curses back down his throat.

His teeth clenched, Nikolas got his feet underneath him and launched himself forward again. Then he drove his fist into the Bolian's bifurcated face.

Hanta staggered back a couple of steps, and bellowed with rage and surprise. But before he could strike back, Nikolas came at him and hit him again, snapping his head around.

And the ensign would have landed a third blow if someone hadn't grabbed his wrist and held it back. Before he knew it, he was being borne to the floor by his crewmates, despite his demands that they release him.

"Nikolas," said a familiar voice, "please stop struggling. There is no need to fight."

The ensign turned and saw Obal looking down at him, his expression one big plea for reason. And with a deep, shuddering breath, Nikolas felt the fight start to go out of him.

"It's all right," he said, his voice sounding distant, like someone else's. "You can let me up now."

"You sure?" someone asked.

"I'm sure," he breathed.

Little by little, he felt the weight lift off him. He got up on one knee and saw that Hanta was being let up as well. The Bolian's nose was leaking dark blood.

And his eyes were still full of fury. But then, he hadn't managed to get a blow in.

Nikolas felt a little pang of satisfaction as he realized he had finally won a fight on the *Stargazer.* But it went away when he saw a trio of security officers crossing the room, headed in his direction.

"What's going on here?" asked Pug Joseph, the sandy-haired acting chief of security.

"Nikolas attacked me," said Hanta, in a tone that could have cut duranium.

Joseph turned to the ensign. "Well?"

Nikolas didn't feel compelled to offer a counter argument. What was the point? Whether he was justified or not, he had gotten into a fight.

And it would cost him. He could hear the captain's words all over again, but this time they had an ominous ring to them. *I would take special care to avoid physical conflicts with your colleagues....*

"I'm waiting," said Joseph, a more patient man than most.

Nikolas shrugged. "It doesn't matter."

Joseph's eyes narrowed. "If that's your statement, I'll put it in my report."

Nikolas didn't object.

Frowning, Joseph took stock of the place. "I'd clean this up if I were you," he told the combatants. Then he led his security officers out of the mess hall.

As Nikolas bent to pick up the debris of his meal, he saw Obal kneel beside him. The Binderian glanced at him with disappointment etched in his features.

After all, Nikolas's chances of a promotion had just diminished to less than nothing. He and his fists had quite effectively seen to that.

Picard had hoped that his newfound companion might know Oblivion better than he did. As it turned out, she knew the place a *lot* better.

It was a good thing, too. As they made their way from hulk to increasingly obscure and dilapidated hulk, the captain saw a number of Steej's blue-and-black security officers, all of them clearly on the prowl for someone.

But Picard always found himself looking at them through the cluttered window of a curio shop or the translucent EM barrier protecting an exotic liquor emporium. One way or the other, they eluded the Rythrian's dragnet.

Sometimes it required the exertion of a dash from one place to another. Sometimes they had to move so slowly and carefully that it seemed they would never get anywhere.

Finally, Picard's companion guided him to a stark-looking hatch with a yellow sign plastered across it. The captain could read only one of the languages in which the sign forbade entrance to the derelict beyond it.

Ignoring the sign, the woman in the hat punched a code into the pad that had been installed beside the door. As it slid open for her, she said, "Come on."

Then she led the way through a poorly lit but otherwise unremarkable airlock to another hatch, which didn't seem to have been secured the same way. That one opened at their approach, revealing a large space that wasn't illuminated any better than the airlock.

It was deserted except for an army of squat, gray containers, perhaps twenty of them sitting on a black metal superstructure while several times that number were scattered about the deck. *A warehouse,* Picard thought, though he couldn't have said what was being stored there.

Not that it mattered. They needed a place to catch their breath and plan their next move, and his companion had obviously found them one.

As Picard followed the woman inside, habit compelled him to identify the structure's origin. Mathenite, he guessed. Or perhaps Pygorian. Both species designed their cargo holds with exposed energy conduits.

As the hatch slid closed behind Picard, his companion wove her way to a place behind a flock of stacked containers and sat down with her back against one of them. Then she gestured for the captain to do the same.

He did as she suggested. Then he took out his "borrowed" phaser and checked its charge. Apparently, the device still had plenty of energy left—though, obviously, the captain hoped he wouldn't need to use it.

The woman took a deep breath, then closed her eyes and let it out. Clearly, their flight from the authorities had worn her out. But then, Picard reflected, any effort was exhausting when a person was carrying a burden to begin with.

And she was most certainly carrying a burden. He just couldn't say what it was.

"What is this place?" he whispered.

His companion opened her eyes and turned her head to look at him. "It was last used as a warehouse. But at the moment, it's...between owners."

The captain looked around. "These containers must have been worth something. I'm surprised the last owner didn't take them with him."

"He probably would have, if he were still alive. Unfortunately, he owed someone a little too much for a little too long."

"Then why didn't that someone seize the containers?"

"Security got to him first."

Picard nodded. "I see." As he regarded the woman, something occurred to him. "If I may ask, how did you know the code to get in here?"

She looked away from him, her eyes glinting with reflected light. "People talk. I listen."

He smiled. "That's it?"

"That's it," she confirmed.

Whether his companion was embellishing the truth or not, Picard was grateful to her. "I'm just glad you didn't *listen* to that Yridian when he accused me of setting off that bomb."

"You have to know whom to listen to," she noted.

Something occurred to him. "If you were so certain of my innocence, why not simply dispute the Yridian's account? It could have simplified the situation immensely."

"Because I know the security forces on Oblivion," the woman said. "It's more important to them to blame someone than to make sure it's the *right* someone. Believe me, my account would have fallen on deaf ears."

"So now," said the captain, "they're after *two* someones."

She looked at him, the slightest, pale hint of amusement in her eyes. "I thought misery loved company."

Picard had to smile at her counter. "It does. But in this case, it wishes it could have escaped without embroiling someone else in my troubles."

"Don't worry," his companion told him. "As I said, I've been in trouble before."

He believed her. Despite the mildness of her manners, she had made quick work of his guard, suggesting that it wasn't the first time she had clunked someone over the head.

"How long do you propose we stay here?" the captain asked.

The woman shrugged. "Until I think of somewhere else to go, I suppose." Her eyes narrowed. "Why? Are you in a hurry?"

"I have to find someone," he explained. He weighed how much to tell her. "I was supposed to meet him in the plaza, and then that bomb went off."

She frowned. "We can worry about that tomorrow, after we've gotten some rest."

Picard didn't like the idea of waiting that long, but he had to admit that it made sense to lie low. And he *was* in need of some sleep.

"As you say," he told his companion.

"By the way," she added, "I'll be sleeping here. *You'll* want to sleep over *there*." She jerked her thumb at a spot on the other side of some containers.

The captain smiled at her sense of propriety. "Of course. I mean, I hope you don't think—"

"Thinking's got nothing to do with it," she told him, clearly intending to terminate the conversation.

Picard chuckled to himself. *Quite a character, this—*

It was then that he realized he didn't know his benefactor's name. It was an oversight he felt compelled to correct.

But to find out *her* name, he would be obliged to offer his own—and as much as she deserved his trust, there was too much at stake for him to confide the truth in her.

"Incidentally," he said, "my name's Dixon Hill."

The security guards already knew him that way. Why weave a more tangled web than he had to?

"Hill," she echoed.

A smile seemed to play around the corners of her mouth. For a moment, Picard wondered if he'd had the bad luck to run into a scholar of twentieth-century detective fiction out here, past the bounds of Federation space—though the odds against that were absurdly long.

"You've heard the name before?" he asked innocently.

Abruptly, even that suggestion of a smile vanished. "No," she told him. "It sounded familiar for a second, but…" Her voice trailed off and her eyes lost their focus again.

The captain said, "And you?"

The woman turned to him. "Guinan."

"Guinan…?" he said, fishing for a last name.

She seemed to consider her response for a long time. Finally she said, in a thin and colorless voice, "Just Guinan."

Chapter Five

LIEUTENANT ULELO, THE NEWCOMER in the *Stargazer's* communications section, allowed himself to be ushered down the corridor that led to the ship's observation lounge.

"Come on," said Emily Bender. "It's supposed to start any minute now."

"Don't worry," Ulelo told her. "They'll wait for us. They always do."

When he and Emily Bender met, shortly after his arrival on the *Stargazer,* she claimed to have known Ulelo at Starfleet Academy. Ulelo had no recollection of such a thing. But then, he didn't remember *anything* that far back.

In fact, the only thing Ulelo recalled with crystal clarity was his mission. His *secret* mission. And the only way he could carry it out was to avoid distractions like Emily Bender.

As a result, he had tried his best to do that. He had told her he didn't remember her. He had rebuffed her less-than-subtle suggestion that they start an intimate relationship.

But then, through a series of circumstances Ulelo still didn't quite understand, Emily Bender had become his friend—not his lover, as she had originally intended, but someone close to him nonetheless.

And mission or no mission, the com officer had become accustomed to that friendship—not to mention the circle of acquaintances it brought with it, most of whom were at that very moment waiting for him to join them.

As soon as Ulelo and his companion arrived at the door to the lounge, Emily Bender tapped the metal plate located beside it. Immediately, the door slid aside, revealing the half-dozen crew people seated around the room's black oval table.

As Ulelo scanned their faces, he identified each of them in his mind. Pfeffer, a lieutenant in the security section. Kochman, the junior navigation officer. Ensign Kotsakos. Transporter operator Vandermeer. Iulus and Urajel, both currently assigned to engineering.

"Well," said Iulus as Ulelo and Bender took the only empty seats in the room, "look who's here. We thought we were going to have to send a search party out for you."

"That's right," said Kotsakos, a slender woman with black hair drawn into a bun. "If we have to listen to

Sulak's Concerto for Harp and Flute, *you* have to listen to it too."

That got a laugh from the group.

"I was detained in the science section," Emily Bender explained, "running extra diagnostics to get ready for the anomaly. And Ulelo was kind enough to wait for me."

"Quite the gentleman, that Ulelo," said Vandermeer.

Again, everyone laughed. But it wasn't a mocking laugh. It was gentle, the kind of laugh shared by comrades.

"Hey," said Pfeffer, a stocky, blond-haired woman, "the gang's all here. What are we waiting for?"

Iulus, who was inserting a chip into the holographic projector in the center of the table, shot Pfeffer a glance. "As I recall, I had to drag you in here kicking and screaming a few weeks ago. Or was that some other blond security officer?"

Nearly a month earlier, when the *Stargazer* was at Starbase 32, Iulus had purchased a series of performances by the London Symphony Orchestra recorded on isolinear chip. In order to savor them properly, he had resolved to play them one a week.

At first, only Kochman and Vandermeer had been inclined to join Iulus for his private concerts in the lounge. But little by little, the others—Ulelo and Emily Bender included—had been lured in or otherwise found their way there.

Two weeks ago, they had heard a piece by a Tellarite composer. Then, last week, they had listened to something by a Rigelian. This week was devoted to Sulak—a Vulcan.

"I've been looking forward to this," said Vandermeer. "They say that if you close your eyes, you feel as if you're trekking across Vulcan's Forge."

"Indeed," said Urajel, an Andorian, "and I heard it said of the Tellarite piece that you feel as if you're slogging through Beggerin Marsh. But I felt no such thing."

"You didn't like the Tellarite piece?" asked Kochman. "I thought *everyone* liked it—even our pal Ulelo, and he's not easy to please."

"Yes," said Vandermeer. "It's the rare composition that gets the Ulelo stamp of approval."

Kotsakos turned to Iulus, who had finished inserting the chip into the holoprojector and was taking his seat. "Speaking of approval," she said, "how do you like engineering?"

Iulus had embarked from Earth with the *Stargazer* as a security officer. It was only after Captain Picard took command of the ship that Iulus asked for and received a transfer to the engineering section.

"I like it," said Iulus, as he turned down the lights. "It's keeping me on my toes."

"More so than security?" Pfeffer asked, feigning astonishment.

"Hey," Iulus said generously, "security was great. I just wanted something a little more—"

"Don't say it," a wincing Emily Bender warned him.

"—stimulating," Iulus finished.

Kochman rolled his eyes. "He said it."

Pfeffer leaned forward in her chair like a she-wolf who had caught the scent of her prey. "More stimulating, is it? Let's see you say that when I'm beaming down to some uncharted planet with an away team and you're up here running diagnostics on the starboard plasma injectors."

That got a grin out of everyone except Urajel, who as an Andorian wasn't inclined to do much grinning. Even Iulus had to smile, conceding that the security officer had scored a point with her remark.

"Fair enough," he told Pfeffer. "But how are you going to feel when I'm examining alien technology on some mysterious, abandoned ship and you're recharging phasers in the armory?"

This time, everybody at the table laughed. Even Urajel seemed vaguely amused at the exchange, though Ulelo wouldn't have staked his life on it.

It was like this almost every day. Banter. Stories of personal achievement and failure. Encouragement. Good-natured gibes. And though Ulelo didn't take part in it as much as Emily Bender and her friends did, he would have been a liar if he said he didn't enjoy it.

And it wasn't just the conversation in which he took pleasure. It was the people—regardless of which crewmen Emily Bender associated with on any given day. He liked them all. He liked being among them. He liked feeling as if he were part of them, and they a part of him.

Just then, the holoprojector conjured a miniature orchestra in black tuxedos. Iulus shushed everyone to silence. And a moment later, music began to issue forth.

The melody was as eerie as it was ethereal, a variety

of stringed instruments and pipes evoking a desert with a harsh, unyielding wind racing through it. Ulelo saw now what Vandermeer meant by her reference to Vulcan's Forge.

He looked about in the light thrown off by the holographic projections and saw enjoyment on the faces of his companions. Had he been able to see his own face, it would no doubt have looked the same.

Ulelo basked in the moment. He savored it. He savored everything about it.

He knew that such feelings could jeopardize the success of his mission. But he couldn't help it. The company of others felt too good for him to give it up.

Even though he knew he couldn't enjoy it forever.

Strange, Guinan thought, as she considered the slumbering specimen of humanity she had rescued from Steej's detention facility. *How very strange.*

The first time she had encountered this "Dixon Hill" fellow, they were in a place called San Francisco at the tail end of Earth's nineteenth century. She remembered him as a balding but distinguished-looking—and yes, unexpectedly charming—individual.

And she remembered also the way he had stared at her then, as if he already knew her.

As Guinan would find out a bit later, he *did* know her—knew her quite well, in fact. In the twenty-fourth century, they would serve together on a starship called *Enterprise,* along with people named Data, Riker, Troi, La Forge, and Crusher.

Apparently, "Hill" was the captain of that twenty-fourth-century vessel. However, he had gone back in time to oppose the Devidians, a time-traveling species that had infested San Francisco in order to steal neural energy from the city's multitude of cholera victims.

And his name wasn't Hill, no matter what he currently wanted her to believe. It was Picard.

He looked younger now than when she had seen him in San Francisco, and not just because he had a full head of hair. He seemed more energetic, more dynamic, more animated. But he also seemed more naïve in a way.

Guinan didn't think the older Picard would have fallen into the trap in the plaza as easily as his younger version did. She felt confident that with the benefit of long experience, he would have sniffed the trap out somehow.

She wondered where he was in the course of his career. Her guess was that he had already joined the fleet to which his *Enterprise* belonged—or *would* belong, since Picard's *Enterprise* probably hadn't been built yet. However, he looked too fresh-faced to have been made a captain.

A subordinate, then, Guinan decided. A lieutenant or some such thing. And more than likely, he was here in Oblivion on official business, which had been rudely interrupted when the bomb went off in the plaza.

She took unexpected comfort in watching the fellow sleep. And these days, her comforts were few and far between.

But then, it was hard not to like him, hard not to care what happened to him. He was so earnest, so obviously intent on doing the right thing.

And he had been so grateful when she got him out of the detention facility, so amazed at her generosity. After all, who in her right mind would take that kind of risk for a complete and utter stranger?

Guinan sighed. Who *indeed*.

She wished she could tell Picard that he *wasn't* a stranger—that the "tough spot" she had mentioned had taken place back in San Francisco, and that she had escaped it by virtue of *his* willingness to take a risk for *her*.

She closed her eyes and tried to retrieve the images. It wasn't difficult, though she had lived a long life and had acquired a great many memories.

Guinan had followed Picard and his people into a cave beneath the city, in search of his Commander Data's head—a rather long and complex story in itself. But as events unfolded, each more curious than the other, she cracked her skull against a rocky outcropping and was knocked unconscious.

It was then that Picard's Devidian adversary fled the cavern through a glowing portal—actually a conduit through time. Unaware of her injury, the team from the *Enterprise* gathered to follow the Devidian through.

Guinan remembered their eagerness, the hard, determined looks in their eyes. And their voices, stretched taut with urgency, as they echoed in the eerie confines of the cave.

But she was bleeding profusely. Without help, she would probably have died in that place.

Luckily for her, Picard was more perceptive than his comrades. As he prepared to follow them through the portal, he caught a glimpse of Guinan and realized how badly she was hurt.

So instead of vanishing along with his officers, he remained there in the cave with her. He knew he might be giving up any chance of returning to his proper time, but it didn't matter. Her survival was more important to him.

When Guinan woke, she saw Picard sitting there beside her. He had bandaged her head with a strip of cloth and stopped the bleeding, effectively saving her life.

While she managed to stay conscious, she expressed surprise that he had stayed to help her. After all, he had stranded himself in the process, cut himself off from everything and everyone he had ever known.

Guinan remembered exactly how he had answered her, word for word. She could hear it now, precisely as she had heard it then: *"I can't very well let anything happen to you. You're far too important to me."*

And he had smiled as he said it.

Then, as Guinan began to lapse into darkness again, she had asked Picard if the two of them were destined to become friends. And he had said of their relationship in that distant future, "It goes beyond friendship."

But she would have to wait nearly five hundred years to learn any more than that. And when the time came that she was finally enlightened, she would be confronted with the *real* irony—the real twist in the weft of their relationship.

Because when Guinan came to understand what Picard meant, when she finally came to appreciate the depth of their friendship, it would be *her* turn to wax cryptic.

And for good reason.

After all, Time could be as volatile as a *mugato,* and as treacherous as a Rigelian ring serpent. It wasn't a thing to be tampered with or taken lightly.

Or rejected, she thought with a pang of loss.

If Guinan revealed too soon what had happened in that cave beneath San Francisco, she would throw everything off for Picard. She would warp the portion of his life that he had yet to make for himself—the joys and the tragedies and the triumphs he had yet to experience, all of which would conspire to make him the man she had known.

And would know again, if all went as it should.

It wasn't just a matter of withholding the details of their first meeting from him. Guinan couldn't even tell him that such a meeting had taken place. She had to keep it all a secret, no matter how much it had meant to her at the time, no matter how critical it had been to her survival.

Simply put, Picard couldn't be allowed a glimpse of his future. Because if he knew too much about it, that future might not come to pass.

And after what he had done for her back in the nineteenth century, he deserved to have the future of prestige and accomplishment that he would earn for himself.

It's funny, Guinan thought. Until she saw Picard sit

down at that bar, she hadn't *wanted* anything—but now she did. Suddenly, she had a goal in life, something she needed to do.

It didn't entirely lift her out of the malaise in which she had been languishing day after day, bereft of joy for so long she couldn't bear to think about it. She had her doubts that anything would accomplish that, ever.

But at least for a little while, her life had a purpose again, and that in itself was something to be thankful for.

Chapter Six

AT THAT PARTICULAR MOMENT, as Admiral Arlen McAteer sat there in the third row of the San Francisco Bay Theater, he didn't have much confidence in Mister William Shakespeare.

He had decided to attend this production of Shakespeare's *Macbeth* only because he had heard good things about it back at headquarters. But the show was almost over, and he hadn't found a great deal to admire about it.

McAteer didn't like what he had heard from the three witches. He appreciated even less the sentiments of Shakespeare's long parade of ghosts. And as the actors playing Prince Malcolm and his noble allies rushed onto the corpse-littered stage, McAteer had a feeling he wasn't going to love what *they* had to say either.

All anybody seemed to want to talk about were the

mistakes Macbeth had made. But to the admiral's way of thinking, they weren't mistakes at all.

So the guy was ambitious. Since when was that a bad thing? Ambition was what had gotten McAteer his admiral's stripes, and ambition was what would propel him to the top spot in all of Starfleet before long.

The admiral knew his history. The situation hadn't been all that different in Shakespeare's time. People didn't get ahead unless they pushed a little. So what was Shakespeare so ticked off about?

Probably somebody had beaten the guy out of a job. Somebody named Macbeth, maybe. And from then on, he had it in for people with initiative.

That was it, McAteer concluded on a note of satisfaction. Shakespeare was just jealous.

Meanwhile, on the stage, Prince Malcolm was looking worried as he stared off into some imagined distance. "I would," he said, "the friends we miss were safe arrived."

Siward, an old fellow with a thick, gray beard, had his eyes on the bodies lying about the stage. "Some must go off," he said soberly. "And yet, by these I see, so great a day as this is cheaply bought."

Malcolm looked back at Siward. "Macduff is missing," he said. "And your noble son."

Siward's jaw fell. Obviously, thought McAteer, in light of what he had just heard, the old guy was reconsidering how cheaply the day had been bought.

Ross, another of Malcolm's pals, put his hand on Siward's shoulder. "Your son, my lord, has paid a soldier's debt. He only lived but till he was a man, the which no sooner had his prowess confirmed in the unshrinking station where he fought, but like a man he died."

Not too many characters got out of these Elizabethan tragedies alive. McAteer had learned that much, at least.

"Then he is dead?" asked Siward.

"Aye," said Ross with a sigh, "and brought off the field. Your cause of sorrow must not be measured by his worth, for then it hath no end."

"Had he his hurts before?" asked Siward.

"Aye," said Ross, "on the front."

McAteer saw where their conversation was going. And for once, he found himself approving of it.

"Well, then," said Siward, "God's soldier be he! Had I as many sons as I have hairs, I would not wish them to a fairer death. And so his knell is knolled."

"He's worth more sorrow," said Malcolm, "and that I'll spend for him."

"He's worth no more," Siward insisted. "They say he parted well and paid his score. And so God be with him!"

Maybe I was wrong, McAteer allowed. *Maybe Shakespeare's going to surprise me and give Macbeth the nod after all.*

Suddenly, Siward looked across the stage. "Here comes newer comfort," he said.

It was then that Macduff came out, carrying a pole in his hand. And what should be perched on the top of it...but Macbeth's bloody, staring head?

The admiral made a sound of exasperation and saw several pairs of eyes turn in his direction. Scowling, he sat back in his seat and tried to keep his frustration to himself.

Crossing the stage, MacDuff presented Malcom with his trophy and said, "Hail, King, for so thou art!"

McAteer rolled his eyes. The guy who deserved to be king was looking down at them from the top of Macduff's pole. Malcolm was a little wimp by comparison.

"Behold," Macduff continued, "where stands the usurper's cursed head. The time is free. I see thee compassed with thy kingdom's pearl, that speak my salutation in their minds—whose voices I desire aloud with mine."

The whole damned thing is a load of hooey, the admiral told himself. *A waste of time.* He couldn't wait to see his colleagues back at headquarters and ask them what in blazes they had seen in this fiasco.

"Hail, King of Scotland!" bellowed Macduff.

"King of Scotland, hail!" Malcolm's other pals replied.

Malcolm looked like a guy who had hit the jackpot but was trying not to show it. "We shall not spend a large expanse of time..." he began.

And I'll spend even less, McAteer thought, as he got up from his seat, sidestepped his way to the aisle, and made a hasty exit to beat the crowd.

Making his way across the lobby, he marveled at his luck. He had hoped this evening would be a distraction from his more serious concerns, of which he had many. Unfortunately, it hadn't worked out that way.

But then, some problems just didn't seem to want to go away. They lingered like bits of bad dreams. And one of those problems was Jean-Luc Picard.

The admiral still didn't think Picard was capable of commanding a starship. As far as he was concerned, the man was too green, too inexperienced. Had McAteer been in charge of this sector when the *Stargazer* returned to Earth, he would never have approved Picard's promotion.

But he wasn't placed in charge until a couple of weeks later. And by then Admiral Mehdi, one of his colleagues, had already plunked Picard down in the *Stargazer's* center seat.

If Picard had been the only puzzle in McAteer's life, it would have been bad enough. However, the sector with which the admiral had been entrusted was quickly becoming a cauldron bubbling with interstellar politics.

With the Ubarrak, the Cardassians, and any number of smaller players angling for position, armed conflict of some sort seemed inevitable. Certainly, the Federation thought so, or it wouldn't have beefed up the number of ships at McAteer's disposal.

When such powerful civilizations clashed, everything was placed in jeopardy. Lives were lost. Cities were destroyed. And all too frequently, careers were dashed on the rocks of unfortunate command decisions.

McAteer was determined not to let that happen to him—not after he had worked so hard to climb through the ranks of the fleet. But he wasn't satisfied to merely stay out of trouble. He meant to leverage the situation to his advantage, so when the last shot was fired and the dust cleared, he would look even better than he had when the battle started.

With that thought in mind, the admiral walked out of the climate-controlled theater into the grasp of the city's cool, moist air. The lights of San Francisco were dazzling, drowning out the stars.

Nonetheless, it was the panoply of stars that drew his gaze. After all, that was where his opportunity lay.

If I play my cards right, McAteer told himself, *this bit of interstellar strife can turn out to be a godsend. It can propel me to the top, even sooner than I had planned.*

But that would only happen if he was alert—if he recognized, secured, and made use of every possible advantage. So for the last few months, he had kept his ear to the ground.

Finally, he had heard something—an overture from a Zartani with a wealth of Ubarrak tactical data. McAteer knew that he had to have what the Zartani was offering. It was just what he needed to give the Federation a leg up on her adversaries.

But there was an irony involved—one that would undoubtedly have impressed the hell out of Shakespeare—because the Zartani wasn't willing to trust just anybody. He wanted to work with one officer and one officer only.

And who, of all people, was that officer? Who held the key that would unlock the Zartani's treasure chest? The admiral grimaced as if he had just eaten a piece of rotten meat.

Who else...but Jean-Luc Picard?

Now, there's was a dramatic turn, McAteer told himself. *There's was a twist of fate worth waxing eloquent about.* His advancement depended not on Denton Greenbriar or some other paragon of Starfleet captaincy, but on the very officer the admiral had been trying to get rid of.

But unlike Macbeth, McAteer intended to have the last laugh. When the dust cleared and the play was over, it would be Picard's head on the pole, and the admiral marching around with it like a kid with a new toy.

"That's right," he said out loud, savoring the image. "Like a kid with the best toy of all."

And for the first time that night, Arlen McAteer smiled.

The Cardassian the others respectfully called "glinn" drew in a deep, calming breath. *I will not show my anger,* he promised himself. *Not to mere underlings.*

They stood in front of him in their rented suite of rooms, a dozen of his fellow Cardassians with their eyes wide in their ridged, scaly orbits, waiting to see their leader's reaction to the news. But the glinn wouldn't give them the pleasure of hearing him curse.

He hadn't risen through the ranks by giving rein to his emotions. He had been careful to submerge his feelings and consider his actions with cold detachment, leading his superiors to believe that he was older than his years.

And he wasn't about to diverge from that policy now by letting his anger fly unrestrained.

Instead, he turned back to his second-in-command and said, in a voice of tempered iron, "Repeat that, Merant. But this time, speak a bit more slowly."

Merant, who was taller and broader than the glinn but not half as shrewd, did as he was told. "The Starfleet captain has escaped from the Second Quadrant Detention Center. Our informant in the security force says the escape was carried out with the assistance of a confederate."

The glinn nodded. "A female, I believe you said. A *human*-looking female."

"Yes, Glinn," came Merant's response.

The glinn wasn't pleased. He wasn't pleased at *all*.

After all, he had known about the human's rendezvous for some time. The army of spies the Cardassians maintained on the Zartani homeworld had seen to that.

In fact, they had been keeping tabs on Demmix ever since his family was killed by the Ubarrak, in the hope that the combination of the Zartani's wealth and his despair would spur him to do something interesting.

And eventually, it had.

It had spurred him to steal Ubarrak tactical data. And it had spurred him to give that information to the Federation, on the condition that he be granted asylum.

The Cardassians knew all that, and a lot more. They knew that Demmix was to meet his old acquaintance, Jean-Luc Picard, and that their meeting was to take place in the traders' maze known as Oblivion.

They even knew what Picard looked like. The Cardassian government had had the foresight to maintain a rather extensive file on Starfleet's commanding officers—including the likeness of every one whose image had ever appeared on the viewscreen of a Cardassian vessel.

The only thing they didn't know was that Demmix would have his appearance altered. It was the glinn who finally came to that conclusion, after several Zartani had arrived in Oblivion in the weeks prior to the rendezvous and none of them had matched Demmix's description.

Unfortunately, the glinn hadn't had the luxury of waiting until the rendezvous took place and then seizing both Picard and Demmix. If he had tried that, the two of them might have given him the slip somehow, or invoked the aid of the city's security force. And then the Cardassians would have come away empty-handed.

So he had taken a more proactive approach to the matter—by secreting a bomb in the plaza, and putting a simple plan into motion. When his operatives saw Picard and a Zartani approaching each other at the agreed-upon place and time, they were supposed to detonate the explosive.

If all went well, Picard would perish in the blast. The glinn's operatives would seize Demmix—and his secrets—in the confusion that was sure to follow.

The glinn had even had a backup plan in place. It involved a hired Yridian "witness," who would accuse the human of detonating the bomb in case he survived the blast.

It had all seemed so clean, so foolproof, right up to the point when the bomb went off. Then, somehow, everything had fallen apart.

The glinn had been reluctant to show his face in the vicinity of the blast, lest he be implicated in it and arrested. But then, that was what underlings were for.

Merant and three others had been deployed in the plaza. Their job was to keep track of any Zartani who showed up at the appointed time, and then grab him as soon as the bomb went off. Not a very difficult task.

And yet, Demmix had managed to slip through their fingers. Worse, the blast had failed to injure Picard. And though the glinn's backup scheme had worked well enough, landing the human in the local detention center, it now seemed that Picard had found his way out again.

Thanks to an ally who had—no doubt—been on hand all along, ready to help him in case anything went wrong.

The glinn bit the inside of his mouth. *I should have thought of that possibility,* he told himself. It nettled him that he had been so handily outmaneuvered.

His eyes narrowed as he regarded Merant. "Tell me about this human-looking female."

Merant blinked—an unmistakable sign of discomfort in a Cardassian. "She had dark skin. A gray dress. And she wore an unusual hat."

The glinn could feel his anger boiling into his throat as a mental picture of the woman emerged. "And that's all you know about her?"

Merant blinked again. "Yes, Glinn."

"That's wonderful," said the glinn, allowing his voice to take on an edge that would cut duranium. "Just wonderful."

There were a great many human-looking females in Oblivion, a number of them with dark skin. As for the hat and the dress...that could be changed easily enough.

Much like Demmix's appearance.

Fortunately, thanks to his spies on the Zartani homeworld, he had other information at his disposal. He knew what Demmix was like, and what his habits were. And though his men hadn't been able to grab the Zartani, they had gotten a glimpse of his surgically altered face in the plaza.

But with Picard on the loose, the Cardassians wouldn't be the only ones looking for Demmix. Much to his disgust, the glinn had a competition on his hands.

He had come here to seize Demmix and find out what he knew. But at the very least now, he had to keep Demmix's information out of Picard's grasp.

Otherwise, the Federation would enjoy an immense advantage in this sector. No longer having to worry about the Ubarrak, it would be able to redeploy more of its resources to the borders of the Cardassian Union.

And that would be bad—not only for Cardassia, but for the glinn himself. His superiors wouldn't look kindly on him for permitting such a distasteful state of affairs.

Just as the glinn wasn't looking kindly on his second-in-command at the moment.

"Merant," he said, "I would like a word with you in private." He took the others in at a glance. "The rest of you are dismissed. Report to your assigned locations."

The glinn waited for them to leave. When the last one had filed out of the room, he turned to Merant again.

"I know," said the glinn, "that the human's escape from the detention facility was not your fault."

Merant obviously hadn't expected sympathy from his superior. It seemed to catch him off-guard.

"Nor is it your fault," the glinn continued, "that he had an accomplice waiting for him here in Oblivion."

Merant seemed to relax.

Which was just what the glinn had wanted him to do. It would make what he had to say next that much more memorable.

"However," the glinn noted in the same reasonable voice, "it is very *much* your fault that Demmix is at large."

Merant's jaw seemed to become unhinged.

"So," said the glinn, "if the humans find Demmix before we do, and spirit him out of Oblivion, you will be held accountable—first of all, by Central Command."

Merant started blinking again.

"I don't envy anyone who's held accountable by Central Command," the glinn told him. "Not in the least. On the other hand, a few of them have survived to lead useful lives, insofar as that is physically possible."

Merant's jaw muscles bunched.

"But it's not just Command that will hold you accountable, you see—because I will hold you accountable as well." The glinn fixed the other man on the spit of his gaze. "And what I will do to you will make Command's response look like a joke."

Merant swallowed.

"Is that clear?" asked the glinn, a dark but subtle promise of violence in his tone.

"Yes," said Merant. "Very clear."

The glinn smiled, though he was far from amused by the situation. "Good. I wouldn't want there to be any misunderstandings between us. You may go now."

Merant inclined his head. Then he turned and left, no doubt eager to be out of his superior's sight.

The glinn nodded, satisfied that he had gotten his message across. Merant would find the Zartani before Picard could, one way or another.

Or, thought the glinn, *my name isn't Enabran Tain.*

Ensign Cole Paris stood in front of the door to his colleague's quarters and waited for the sensor mechanism to announce his presence.

Like Paris, his colleague was an ensign, relatively new to the *Stargazer* and Starfleet in general. But that was where the similarity between them ended.

Paris was human, of medium height and medium

ld, with fair hair and what had been described to him
ooyish features. He was also the latest entry in a long
of Parises, several of his closest relatives occupying
ominent place in the lore of the Fleet.

His colleague, on the other hand, had no height or
ld, no hair, and no real facial features—though she
ld project the illusion of features through the trans-
ent faceplate in the special containment suit she
re.

She also wasn't human, or even solid. She was a
hrak, a low-density being whose species had evolved
he upper atmosphere of a gas giant—which was why
had to squeeze her mass into the containment suit.
hout it, it would have been impossible for her to
ve through the ship, much less interact with moni-
s, control panels, and her crewmates.

Unfortunately, the suit was difficult for Jiterica to
trol. However, she had been getting more expert at it
r the course of the last few weeks.

Coincidentally, it was in those same few weeks that
is and Jiterica had become friends.

t was something he would never have envisioned in a
lion years. After all, when he first beamed aboard, he
n't known what to make of the Nizhrak. She was so
sual, so different from anyone he had ever met.

Then Commander Wu had asked them to work to-
er to rescue a research vessel called the *Belladonna,*
ch had gotten itself caught in a strange, deadly space
maly.

n order to save both ship and crew, Jiterica had
ced her life in Paris's hands. And he had found the

courage to come through for her, overcoming a deep-rooted emotional problem in the process.

For a while after that, their schedules had conspired to keep them from seeing each other. Then they had met unexpectedly in a corridor near Paris's quarters, and Paris had promised to get together with her.

In fact, he called on her just as soon as his shift that day was over. But then, Starfleet's Parises were known for keeping their promises.

That first time, Paris and Jiterica had just lounged in her quarters and talked. The next one, they took a walk together through some of the ship's less-traveled corridors.

Each time, they got to know each other a little better. And Paris found that the more he knew about Jiterica, the more he *wanted* to know.

It hardly mattered to him anymore that they had risked their lives together. What mattered was how much they enjoyed each other's company.

It was in that spirit that Paris was calling on Jiterica now. The other times, he had called ahead first. But this time, he wanted it to be a surprise.

After all, as his aunt Patricia had often told him, spontaneity was the secret of life. And he hadn't known too many people smarter than his aunt Patricia.

But the longer Paris stood in front of Jiterica's quarters, the more he began to see that spontaneity had its downside. After what had to be a full two minutes, his friend still hadn't answered the door.

The ensign didn't understand. He hadn't asked the ship's computer to determine Jiterica's whereabouts

re than five minutes ago, and the computer had said
:quivocally that she was in her quarters.

Strange, he thought.

Maybe the sensor mechanism had stopped working. It
n't happen very often, but it was a possibility. To cir-
nvent the problem, Paris touched the pressure-sensitive
te located on the bulkhead, next to the doors.

:till no answer.

The ensign frowned. Maybe he had miscommunicated
h the computer somehow. He decided to try it again.

"Computer," he said, looking up at the intercom grid
den in the ceiling, "where is Ensign Jiterica?"

The reply came in a pleasant, feminine voice. "En-
n Jiterica is in her quarters."

Paris's frown deepened. Something was wrong.

With all Jiterica's physical differences and the suit
· was forced to wear, it wasn't difficult to imagine that
· had gotten herself into trouble somehow—or that it
s something she couldn't deal with on her own.

f that were the case, and she was rescued by a bunch
security officers, it would be a source of great embar-
sment to her. And the last thing Jiterica needed, now
t she was finally beginning to fit in with the crew, was
)ther embarrassment to live down.

Paris knew an override code from the rotation he had
nt in security, shortly after he came on board. If Mis-
Joseph hadn't changed the code, he might be able to
into Jiterica's quarters without anyone knowing.

)f course, if he were wrong, it would be a violation
Jiterica's privacy—and a serious one, at that. But he
compelled to take the chance.

Quickly but carefully, Paris tapped the code into a strip below the pressure-sensitive plate. For a moment, he thought Joseph had changed the code after all, or maybe he had tapped it in incorrectly.

Then the door slid open, revealing the contents of Jiterica's quarters. Without hesitation, Paris took a step inside and looked around. But he didn't see Jiterica. What he saw was a strange, iridescent mist, filling the room from wall to wall.

At first, Paris recoiled, thinking there was a plasma leak somewhere. But that didn't make sense. There weren't any conduits in this part of the ship.

Besides, the mist wasn't hot. In fact, it felt like tiny pieces of ice as it brushed against his skin. Tiny pieces of ice *that were speaking to him*...

Not in words, but in a language he understood nonetheless. A language that went directly to his brain and spoke of unimaginable freedom, of easy trust and camaraderie, of a place so beautiful his senses couldn't begin to embrace it...

Of *home*.

How was this possible? he asked himself. How could he be feeling such things?

Then, through the twinkling, shifting mist, Paris caught a glimpse of Jiterica. She was lying limply on the bed in the next room—unconscious, or maybe something worse. His heart pounding, he moved toward her, wondering what had happened and how he could help her.

But when he reached Jiterica, he saw that her suit was lying flat and open, and that the ghostly visage he was used to seeing through the faceplate of her helmet wasn't there. That's when it occurred to him that the suit was empty.

And that Jiterica was somewhere else.

Paris had already begun to ask himself *where* when he realized he already held the answer. As if in confirmation, the mist stabbed at his cheek with its icy, pinprick touch.

My god, he thought. *It's her.*

The mist was Jiterica...and it was all around him, enveloping him, taking him into itself as if he were part of it. He had never felt anything even remotely like it.

Then he realized that it wasn't just touching his skin. He was *breathing* it. He was taking it inside himself, blurring the boundaries where the mist ended and he began.

It felt wrong to Paris. Or rather, it felt right. *Too* right.

The thoughts he was sharing with her, the feelings, the intimacy...it was too much, too sudden. He wasn't prepared for it. And though it was *her* privacy he was invading, it was Paris who felt naked and exposed.

Get out, he told himself. *Now.*

Finding the doorway through the sparkling waves of mist, Paris bolted for it. The duranium panels slid open for him just as he shot through them, hoping to escape.

And escape he did. The mist hung back inside the limits of Jiterica's quarters, separating itself from him, relinquishing its unspoken claim on him.

Paris felt a wave of relief. But he also felt something else—an eerie sense of loss.

And as he made his way down the corridor, he felt a third thing. After all, he had invaded Jiterica's self, perhaps even *violated* her in some uniquely Nizhrak sense.

The ensign hadn't intended to do that. All he had

meant to do was *help* her. But despite his good intentions, he might have hurt her to the core of her being.

And if he had, he could never take it back. It would haunt him the rest of his days.

What have I done? he thought.

Suddenly, it occurred to him that he might be compounding his invasion by running away. If he had injured Jiterica as he feared, she might be in need of someone to console her—someone to be with her.

Or would his coming back only make things worse?

Paris didn't know. He couldn't *possibly* know. Jiterica wasn't anything like him.

Nonetheless, he had stopped and was about to return to her quarters when he realized he wasn't alone in the corridor. Someone was coming after him.

It was Jiterica. But this time, she was wearing her containment suit. And she was moving as quickly and purposefully as he had ever seen her move.

What does she want? Paris wondered. He dreaded the prospect of finding out.

Chapter Seven

PARIS STEELED HIMSELF as he watched Jiterica lumber toward him in her containment suit, her ghostly features visible through her transparent faceplate.

Normally, she made those features reflect what she was feeling, so she could better communicate with the humanoids around her. But at the moment, her expression was blank—chillingly so.

It was if Jiterica had lost the desire to make herself appear human. Or maybe what she was feeling was just so intense that she couldn't translate it.

Either way, it wasn't a good sign.

Still, Paris stood there and waited for her. After what he had done, he *had* to.

Finally, Jiterica caught up with him. They stood face-to-faceplate, his flesh-and-blood eyes locked on her spectral ones. He opened his mouth to apologize, to beg her forgiveness.

But before he could do that, she spoke first. And what she said, in the tinny, artificial voice that her suit afforded her, was "I'm sorry."

Paris looked at her. *She* was sorry? "For what?"

"For…" She hesitated. "For what happened in my quarters. I didn't think it would be a problem if I came out of my suit for a few minutes."

He didn't know what to say.

Jiterica seemed to search for words. "It's just that it's so difficult to live *inside* something."

"I'm sure it is," he responded numbly.

"If I had known you were going to come in—"

"I shouldn't have—"

"I thought the door—"

"I was afraid you were in trouble, or I—"

Their words tumbled over each other's, making the entire mess unintelligible. Suddenly, they stopped and looked at each other, each reluctant to speak lest he or she interrupt the other.

Finally, it was Jiterica who broke the silence—even though she was the newcomer in terms of spoken communication. "I just wanted you to know that our…contact…was unintentional."

Paris nodded. "On my part as well."

Now the Nizhrak's features *did* take on a humanlike expression. It was one of relief.

"Next time," he promised her, "I'll think twice before barging in."

"And I will never leave my suit again. It was wonderful getting out of it, even for a short time. But getting back in was...torture."

Paris couldn't even imagine.

Existing in a drastically condensed form couldn't have been comfortable for her. But achieving it in the first place had to be...well, Jiterica had said it, hadn't she?

Torture.

"So we have achieved an understanding?" she asked.

Paris smiled at the awkwardness of her question. "Yes. I guess we have."

"Good," said Jiterica. "I would hate to think I had damaged our friendship."

He was touched by her concern. "Don't worry," he assured her. "You didn't."

She continued to look at him. "If I could ask you a favor...?"

"Of course," he said.

"I do not wish anyone else to know what happened just now. The suit and the difficulties I have with it are my problems—no one else's. I can cope with them if it allows me to remain a viable member of the crew."

Paris nodded again. "It'll stay between us."

If her expression was any indication, she was pleased with his response. "Thank you."

He shrugged. "Don't mention it."

Picard woke with a start, not knowing where he was. Then, gradually, it came back to him.

The bomb and his aborted rendezvous. His imprisonment and escape. His slow, careful progress through the orbital city until Guinan finally brought him to—

Guinan, he thought. Where was she?

The captain got up and looked around the container-filled warehouse, but his companion was nowhere in sight. It was hardly a comforting observation.

Has she been captured? he wondered. But if she were, why wouldn't he have been taken as well?

No, Picard told himself. *Not captured.* But she might have left him there for a moment, perhaps to get some food.

No sooner had he completed the thought than he heard a shuffling sound in a corner of the compartment. Dropping out of sight, he picked up his stolen phaser pistol. Then he listened—and heard the shuffling sound again.

It was coming from one of the corners of the room—an area hidden from the captain. Negotiating a path among several stacks of containers, he made his way toward the sound.

Careful, he thought.

He was little more than halfway there when he heard someone say, "Relax. It's just me."

Picard recognized the voice as Guinan's. Taking a deep breath, he renewed his quest until he caught a glimpse of her. She appeared to be kneeling beside something—a much smaller and rounder container than the others in the room, made of what appeared to be white plastiform.

"Can I give you a hand?" he asked.

"I'm fine," Guinan told him.

As the captain joined her, he noticed that one of the larger containers was open, its lid flipped up and back. Peering inside it, he saw a number of other small containers, each a different shape and color.

"My food stash," Guinan explained.

Picard nodded. "How convenient."

Obviously, his companion had foreseen the need for a hiding place. For all he knew, she might even have hidden here on some previous occasion.

He watched her close the open container by pressing a stud in its side. Then she picked up the smaller container and slid back a rounded panel, exposing its contents.

"I hope you like *feh'jennek*," Guinan said, referring to a Vobilite foodstuff that would have been indistinguishable from soy cake were it not for its lush, scarlet color.

"Love it," the captain assured her.

"You're lying," she told him as she reached into the container, extracted a healthy chunk of the stuff, and handed it to him. "Actually, I don't like it much either, but it keeps better than most anything else."

He waited until she had taken out a piece for herself. Then the two of them sat down and had their breakfast.

"What made you stock this place with food?" Picard inquired after a while.

Guinan shrugged and looked at the floor. "I need to be alone sometimes—more alone than I can be in a hotel room."

He sensed that she didn't want to say any more than that, so he restrained himself from probing further.

However, her response was of a piece with the sadness he saw in her eyes.

Something had happened to her, he thought, something that affected her to the depths of her soul. Perhaps if they knew each other long enough, she would tell him about it.

But for now, the captain had other concerns on his mind. "That fellow I was supposed to meet…"

"You need to start looking for him, I suppose."

"Yes. It's rather important."

Guinan frowned. "Important enough to risk getting recaptured by security?"

"Yes," said Picard, giving out more information than he cared to. "That important."

She gazed off into the distance. "Steej will have your description posted all over the place. You won't get very far before someone recognizes you."

"I'm sure you're right, " he said. "Nonetheless, I have to make the attempt."

Guinan regarded the human for a moment. Then her brow began to bunch above the bridge of her nose, giving him the impression that she was getting an idea.

"It could work," she said.

"What could?" he asked.

"Everyone will be looking for a human with a healthy head of brown hair and a woman in a big hat. I can always get rid of the hat, but…"

"But what?" he prodded.

"But the *hair*…" she said.

The captain had a feeling he wasn't going to like this.

* * *

Steej walked through the long, scarred hold of an Ajanni freighter that had been turned into a luridly lit bazaar, and studied the faces of everyone gathered there.

Only a handful of them looked human. And of that handful, no one came close to matching the description of the bomber or his female accomplice.

But they were still in Oblivion. The security director was certain of that.

After all, he had sent out detailed descriptions of the fugitives through the city's security net—transmitting them not only to his own officers, but to his counterparts in the city's other sectors as well.

Less than twenty minutes after the prisoner escaped, they had locked the city down. Ships were forbidden to leave until they were searched, lest they contain a couple more passengers than they were supposed to.

Steej winced as he was jostled by a passing Nausicaan, his ribs still sore from the phaser blast he had absorbed. "Watch where you're going," he snapped.

The Nausicaan turned, considered him for a moment, and said, "I will"—the closest thing to an apology that he was likely to utter. Then he continued on his way.

The Rythrian decided to move on as well, albeit in the opposite direction. He had seen enough here. He wanted to inspect the bar two compartments farther down.

Mercantile captains frequented the place when they were looking for cargo to haul. The human and his friend might have gone there to see if they could get a ride out of Oblivion, despite the security crackdown.

It was worth a look, at least. And if there wasn't anything interesting there, Steej had a long list of other locations to check out.

His counterparts in the city's other sections wouldn't have been doing their own legwork on a case. They considered it beneath them.

But Steej had always taken crimes in his part of Oblivion personally, as if he himself were the victim. And in this instance, he had even more reason to do so.

He wasn't normally the vindictive sort, but he didn't like what the human had done to him. Steej wanted very much to get him back in a detention cell, so he could give the human a taste of what he had doled out.

Perhaps several tastes.

It won't be long, he told himself, as he left the bazaar and walked through an exotic-clothing store on his way to the bar. *It won't be long at all.*

Of course, he was dealing with a most clever team here. They had to be clever, or one wouldn't have been able to break the other one out of the detention facility.

But Steej was clever too.

He had yet to meet the fugitive capable of eluding his dragnet—and he doubted that either of these two would become the first. Soon, they would find themselves as overmatched as all the others.

And when that happened, Steej told himself, his ribs would feel a whole lot better.

* * *

Ensign Nikolas emerged from the turbolift, barely even took notice of which officers were on the bridge, and walked past them to the door of the captain's ready room.

Picard wouldn't be inside. He was on a mission somewhere, though the details of it hadn't been widely circulated. But then, it wasn't Picard whom Nikolas had come to see.

The ensign waited for the sensor above the door to register his presence there. Finally, the doors slid open and admitted Nikolas to the captain's inner sanctum.

Ben Zoma, the *Stargazer*'s first officer, was sitting behind Picard's desktop computer, its screen casting a pale green glow on his face. As Nikolas entered the room, Ben Zoma turned to him.

"Pull up a chair," he said, indicating the one across the desk from his own.

Nikolas didn't thank his superior for his consideration. His only response was to sit down.

Ben Zoma regarded him for a moment. Then he said, "I've got a security report here that says you and Mister Hanta were fighting in the mess hall. Can you tell me what was so important that you came to blows over it?"

Nikolas had been anticipating a meeting like this one ever since security got involved in the matter. He shrugged. "It just happened, sir."

Ben Zoma glanced at the monitor screen again. "According to Hanta, you started the fight. Is that true?"

The ensign didn't care to defend himself any more

now than he had in the mess hall. "I guess," he said, "that depends on your point of view."

The first officer leaned back in his chair. "And what's *your* point of view, Mr. Nikolas?"

Nikolas shrugged again. "I upset Hanta's tray. His food spilled on his uniform."

"So you're saying it was an accident?"

"That's right."

Ben Zoma looked puzzled. "Why didn't you mention that to the security team?"

"I guess I didn't think it was important," Nikolas told him.

The first officer nodded. "I see. Tell me, Ensign… have you been having trouble sleeping lately?"

The question caught Nikolas off-guard. Then he remembered seeing Ben Zoma on one of his more recent jaunts.

"A little," he confessed.

"And would that have anything to do with what happened in the mess hall?"

Nikolas really didn't want to talk about it. "I'm not sure what you mean, sir."

But Ben Zoma was relentless. "I think you know *exactly* what I mean, Ensign."

Nikolas squirmed in his chair. Unfortunately, he couldn't leave—not without his superior's permission.

"I'm hearing things I don't like," the first officer said, "and not just from the security section. In the past several days, you've been late for two different shifts and fallen asleep in a third one."

Actually, Nikolas had fallen asleep on *two* occasions—once in engineering and once in sickbay—but he didn't feel compelled to point that out. "I'll try to do better, sir."

Ben Zoma chuckled. "Why don't I believe that? Why do I have the feeling you'll go back to the very same behavior—with maybe another fight thrown in for good measure?"

The ensign didn't have an answer for that. Of course, he wasn't trying very hard to come up with one.

Ben Zoma smiled, but it was clear that he wasn't very happy. "Good officers don't turn into bad ones overnight. There's always a reason for it. And I want to know what it is."

Nikolas shook his head, feigning regret. "I'm sorry, Commander. I can't help you."

"Can't?" the first officer echoed. "Or won't?"

Again, Nikolas fell silent.

Ben Zoma leaned forward across the captain's desk. "Does it have anything to do with Gerda Idun Asmund?"

Nikolas's expression must have betrayed him, because he could see a sense of accomplishment in his superior's.

"I know a *little* about what happens on this ship," said Ben Zoma. "It was no secret that you were infatuated with her. And you've yet to explain how you wound up in the transporter room trying to stop her from abducting Simenon."

Nikolas had gone there with the intention of returning with Gerda Idun to her own universe. It was only chance that had put him in a position to stop her from taking Simenon.

Not for the first time, he cursed the way things had worked out. *Why couldn't it have been* me *she came for? Why couldn't* I *have been the key to her people's survival?*

Ben Zoma looked at him. "Well?"

Nikolas felt a new pang of longing. It happened every time he thought of her. Every single time.

"Gerda Idun is gone," he told Ben Zoma. "There's no point in talking about her."

The first officer regarded him a moment longer, a shadow of sadness crossing his face. Then he said, "Have it your way, Ensign. Dismissed."

Nikolas felt no sense of achievement for having stymied Ben Zoma's attempts to uncover his pain. He felt no rush of victory as he got up and left the room.

All he felt was emptiness.

Picard felt an unaccustomed draft on his scalp.

Afraid that it was coming from an open door, he turned his head in the direction of the storage room's only entrance. But the door to the adjoining cosmetics parlor was closed, a concession to their need for secrecy.

He had barely assured himself of the fact when he felt four strong fingers clamp down on his cranium and rotate it ninety degrees to the right.

"Calm yourself," said a husky, feminine voice.

The captain frowned. "I was only trying to see if—"

"I'm almost done," the voice added.

Suddenly, he felt the robe he had been wearing whisked away from him. Then two viselike hands lifted him off the stool on which he had been sitting.

Guinan, who had been standing off to the side and watching, tilted her head appraisingly. But, ominously, she didn't see fit to say anything.

The captain reached for the top of his head. Somehow, it wasn't quite where he had expected it to be. But then, a significant part of what he usually found there was conspicuous by its absence.

And when he finally *did* find something, it was disquietingly *smooth*.

The next thing he knew, a mirror had been placed in front of him. "What do you think?" asked the same husky, feminine voice, with what struck Picard as excessive enthusiasm.

He couldn't help wincing a little. The complete and utter lack of hair above his eyebrows made him look a great deal like his father—and at the age of twenty-eight, he wasn't at all ready for that.

Thanks to the mirror, the captain could see the female who had depilated his head standing behind him. Like all Dranoon, she had pale green skin, a squarish head on a massive frame, and a thick mane of blue-black hair.

At that particular moment, he envied her the mane.

"It's...different," he told her.

"Actually," said Guinan, "it's a good look for you."

Picard wished he could agree with her.

The Dranoon, whose name was Dahlen, put the mirror down. Then she opened a drawer and took out something that looked like an old-fashioned, Starfleet-issue hypospray. Holding it up to the light of an overhead fixture, she pressed the tiny white buttons in its side in what appeared to be a familiar sequence.

"What are you doing?" the captain asked.

The Dranoon shrugged. "You want to change your appearance, don't you?"

He eyed the device in her powerful green hand. "I thought I already had."

"You still look human," she told him. "I thought you might want to address that."

"And become...what?" Picard wondered.

"A Cataxxan," Guinan replied.

"Exactly," said Dahlen. Then she pressed the device against the captain's neck and released something into him.

He looked at his hand. Something was happening to his skin there. It was slowly but surely becoming darker—and changing color as well.

"Purple suits you," the Dranoon noted, and held up the mirror for him again.

In a matter of moments, the captain saw a Cataxxan looking back at him from the surface of the mirror. He had to admit that the disguise was an effective one. His own mother would have had trouble recognizing him.

"All right," said Dahlen, "you're done." She turned to Guinan. "Your turn now."

Picard took consolation in one thing: no matter how bizarre he felt with his head shaved, Guinan was bound to feel a good deal more so.

He was still thinking that when his benefactor removed her great, gray hat...and showed him a pate every bit as hairless as his own!

"Something wrong?" she asked.

The captain shook his head. "No. Nothing at all."

"Except my head."

He indicated his indifference with a shrug. "Lots of humanoid species are hairless."

"But you didn't expect *me* to be that way."

Picard's first impulse was to protest to the contrary. Then he realized that it would be better if he simply came out with the truth.

"I didn't," he admitted.

"Well," Guinan said, "as it happens, I'm not naturally bald. I've just been through some...interesting times lately."

As she said it, her eyes took on that faraway look again. And this time, there was more pain in them than usual.

Interesting times indeed, the captain thought. And once more, he found himself wondering about the details.

Unfortunately, they were Guinan's business and no one else's. If she wanted to keep them to herself, he had no choice but to accept her decision.

"You don't owe me any explanations," Picard told her.

"Nonetheless," Guinan said as she emerged from her funk, "I thought I'd tell you. You never know what kind of information might prove valuable someday."

"Ready?" asked the Dranoon, wielding her hypospray device a second time.

Guinan smiled a thin, sad smile. "Sure," she said, "go ahead. Turn me purple."

In the next few seconds, that was what her friend did. As the dye spread throughout her body, she and the captain became a matched pair.

"Not bad," Guinan said, inspecting herself in the mirror.

"I agree," Dahlen remarked. "You might want to think about making it permanent."

"I might at that," Guinan told her. Then she turned to Picard. "What do *you* think?"

"What I think," he said, acutely aware of his need to find Demmix, "is that we have a bit of a search ahead of us. And according to an old Earth proverb—"

Guinan held up her hand. "A thousand miles, a single step. I've heard it."

With a word of thanks to her large green friend, she led the way out of the storage room.

Chapter Eight

IT WASN'T THE FIRST TIME Picard had been altered to resemble another humanoid species.

As an ensign, he had undergone superficial surgeries on three separate occasions in order to conduct clandestine surveys of pre-spaceflight civilizations. It wasn't anything unusual. It was simply part of serving in Starfleet.

But this was different, Picard thought, as he made his way through a bazaar of exotic goods located in the hold of an old Anjottu freighter.

He wasn't walking among people who had no reason to look beyond his appearance, no reason to suspect he was anything but what he seemed. Instead, he was rubbing shoulders with keen-eyed merchants, every one of whom knew that a bomb had gone off recently in their vicinity.

He could see it in their eyes. They were on the lookout for the human accused of the crime.

So it wasn't just Steej's security officers the captain and his companion had to worry about. It was *everyone*.

As he thought that, Guinan leaned closer to him and whispered, "For pity sake, *relax*. Stop thinking like a fugitive and you won't look like one."

It was good advice. Picard did his best to follow it.

Not that it was easy. And it became considerably more difficult when he caught sight of a couple of security officers in their blue-and-black uniforms, heading right for the captain and his companion.

But the security officers veered off before they could get too close, apparently to question an Orion beverage merchant. Careful to look straight ahead, Picard walked right past them.

"Breathe," said Guinan.

He couldn't help smiling at the remark—which, he imagined, could only add to the efficacy of his disguise. "I will continue to try," he said.

Suddenly, he saw what they were looking for—a cylindrical black kiosk with the binary-sun symbol of Oblivion's largest passenger line. A Tellarite was standing in front of the kiosk's convex screen, booking passage on one vessel or another.

Picard frowned. "I suppose we will have to be patient."

"Come on," said Guinan. "We'll pretend to be interested in some open-toed sandals until he's done." And she guided her companion over to a shopwindow displaying an eclectic assortment of footwear.

As luck would have it, the Tellarite wasn't long in completing his transaction. As soon as the "Cataxxans" noted his departure, they left the shopwindow and took the Tellarite's place in front of the kiosk.

Its screen showed them the next several flights, their prices, and what accommodations were still available. The topmost flight, which was all but full, left in just under eighteen hours.

Guinan touched the flight number on the pressure-sensitive screen and its itinerary popped up. It included several planets where Demmix could have hidden himself.

None of them were in Federation space. But that wouldn't be a problem as far as Demmix was concerned. All that would matter was his getting out of Oblivion.

It wasn't that the Zartani would be happy to leave the city. After all, he had failed to pass on what he knew about the Ubarrak, and thereby achieve a measure of revenge.

However, his life would soon be forfeit if the Ubarrak found out what he was up to. With rendezvous no longer an option, Demmix would be forced to think of only one thing: survival.

Guinan looked at him. "You're certain your friend would be on this flight?"

Picard nodded. "Reasonably certain."

His companion shrugged. "Then why not just intercept him at the docking port?"

He had already considered the possibility. "I can do that," he said, "if it becomes my only option. However, after what happened in the plaza, the authorities should be paying close attention to departing flights."

Guinan didn't know the whole of the problem, but she seemed to know enough of it. "You're worried that you'll draw their attention," she surmised.

"Yes. Especially since it might take my friend a moment to recognize me."

Also, whoever had set off the bomb in the plaza could arrange to be at the docking port as well. Picard didn't want to invite a second such incident.

Guinan frowned. "Then you've got eighteen hours to get hold of your friend."

"So it would seem," the captain said.

And if he *couldn't,* the Federation would lose the strategically critical information Demmix was carrying.

Picard was determined not to let that happen. He hadn't undertaken this mission to let it slip through his fingers without a fight.

The question was where to start looking for Demmix. Oblivion was a big place, with lots of nooks and crannies, and the Zartani would be doing his best to stay out of sight.

Picard regretted now that he hadn't insisted on a fallback plan. However, Demmix had resisted the idea, saying that he didn't want anyone to know his intentions in the event that the rendezvous went sour.

That way, he couldn't be intercepted even if the captain were caught and interrogated. It had seemed to Picard to be an overly cautious position at the time.

But then, he hadn't really believed that their scheme

would go sour, much less that he would wind up in a detention facility.

Obviously, he had been wrong.

But now he had no way to contact Demmix, no way to let him know that his escape could still take place. It was unfortunate, to say the least.

Still, the captain had the gall to believe that he could salvage the situation.

By then, a Vobilite seemed to be waiting for the kiosk, so Picard and Guinan moved off. But as they did this, the captain was thinking.

All right, he told himself. *Perhaps I cannot communicate with Demmix. But I know him—his likes, his dislikes, his needs. If I know those things, I should also be able to determine his whereabouts, shouldn't I?*

The first idea that came to him was the most obvious. "He's a Zartani," he said out loud. "They have unique needs with regard to respiration."

It was an understatement.

The Zartani homeworld had an atmosphere that was much lower in oxygen and higher in carbon dioxide than that of Earth—and, for that matter, most other worlds that had given rise to sentient humanoids.

Guinan nodded. "I've seen those things they wear on their noses—some of kind of gas-supplement devices."

"Indeed," said Picard. "They cannot survive for more than a few minutes without them. And the devices hold only a limited supply—less than enough to see Demmix through the night."

"So he would have to keep waking up and inserting refills," Guinan noted.

He nodded. "Precisely."

Fortunately, there were hotels in Oblivion that catered to species with special needs. The captain would have been surprised if at least a few didn't cater to Zartani.

"I wonder," Picard said, "how many hotels in this part of Oblivion have Zartani clienteles?"

"I don't know," she replied. "But I can find out."

The hotel registry—another kiosk arrangement—was two old hulks away. When they got to it, Guinan called up the information they were looking for.

"There are three of them," she announced. She moved aside so Picard could see the list on the monitor screen. "Which one do you want to start with?"

Picard pointed to the name at the top of the list. "How about this one?"

Ben Zoma frowned as he sat in the center seat before a viewscreen full of static stars, one of them the brilliant, young sun around which Oblivion and its mother planet revolved. It had been several hours since Picard's scheduled rendezvous with Nuadra Demmix, and they still hadn't heard from him.

"I wonder," said a familiar voice, "if what they say about a watched pot is true of a watched star."

Ben Zoma turned and saw Wu. She hadn't been on the bridge a minute ago. But now she was standing at the first officer's side the way he sometimes stood at the captain's.

"It never boils?" he ventured.

The second officer smiled. "In literal terms, it doesn't work very well. But I think you get the idea."

"I suppose I do," he said.

Wu glanced at the screen. "What do you think happened?"

Ben Zoma shrugged. "Maybe somebody recognized the captain and decided he'd bring a good ransom. Maybe he ran into trouble with some thieves. It could have been any of a hundred things."

The second officer nodded. "Do you still want to wait?"

He could feel his teeth grinding together. *Not for a minute,* he thought. But what he told Wu was "There's more at stake here than the captain's life. I've got to give him a chance to finish what he started."

Even if it means arriving too late to rescue him? Ben Zoma asked himself.

Even then, he answered grudgingly.

"By my count," he said out loud, "he's still got almost sixteen hours." He glanced at Wu. "But you might want to think about putting a team together—in case sixteen hours goes by and we still haven't heard from him."

She nodded. "No sooner said than done." And she left the bridge to carry out his order.

As Picard emerged from a long, unusually narrow airlock into a space that looked as if it had once been a hangar for small vessels, he saw an electronic sign suspended from the high, rounded ceiling.

It communicated something in bold, red Zartani characters. Unfortunately, the captain couldn't read Zartani.

He looked back at Guinan, who had followed him in. "Any idea what that says?" he asked.

She studied the sign for a moment. "The Heavenly Meadow. It's where an ancient teacher earned his divinity by wrestling with an immense, talking worm."

The captain looked at her. "How do you know that?"

She shrugged. "I get around."

By then, they had reached the hotel's front desk, which was situated just beyond the sign. It was smooth, rounded in the front, and fabricated from a ruddy alloy that clashed with the pale silver of the walls.

The fellow sitting behind it was a Zartani. But then, that made sense. After all, he was running an establishment that specialized in Zartani accommodations.

As Picard and Guinan approached the hotel manager, he regarded them with a discernible wariness in his shiny black eyes. But he had to have guessed that neither of them was there to secure a room.

"Can I help you?" he asked, his breath laced with a sharp scent—the product of a seed his people liked to chew.

"I hope so," said Picard. "We're looking for a friend—a Zartani, as it happens. We think he may have spent the night in your establishment."

The Zartani let out a laugh. It was an ugly sound by anyone's standards. "You think I have time to stand here and answer idle questions?" he asked.

He thrust a long, bronze thumb over his shoulder. Following it, Picard saw the corridor full of doors that started just behind the front desk.

"In case you haven't noticed," the Zartani said self-importantly, "I have a hotel to run."

Picard could feel the ripple of muscles in his jaw. There were lives at stake here, his own not the least of them. He would be damned if he was going to let this chortling buffoon withhold the information they needed.

"Now listen here," he said, his voice clipped with frustration. "We haven't come this far to be—"

But before he could finish, Guinan held a hand up in front of him. "What my companion here means," she said in a surprisingly pleasant voice, "is that we're in a bind—and you're the only one in a position to help us out of it."

The hotel manager still looked annoyed, but not quite as much as when he had spoken to Picard. "Didn't you hear me?" he snapped. "I'm too busy."

"I can *see* how busy you are," said Guinan. "A lot busier than any of the other hoteliers we've spoken with. But then, they weren't like you."

That seemed to get the Zartani's attention. "What do you mean?" he asked.

"They didn't even know who was staying in their establishment. Can you imagine that?"

The Zartani made a sound of disdain. "I always know who's in my hotel. I make it my *business* to know."

"That doesn't surprise me in the least," said Guinan. "I knew you were a cut above the other hotel managers as soon as I walked in here."

"You did?" the Zartani asked. It seemed to Picard

that the fellow's cynicism was starting to slip away.

Guinan smiled a cryptic smile. "Sure. But you must hear that all the time."

"Uh...right," said the Zartani, pushing a strand of white hair back from his bronze forehead. "Of course." But it was clear from his tone that he didn't hear it at all.

"I bet that's the reason you're so busy," Guinan said. "And so successful. Because you don't just put in the minimum effort. You go the extra mile."

"I do," the Zartani agreed, hanging on Guinan's words as if they were drops of cool water in the midst of an otherwise parched desert.

"It's the way you were brought up—to work harder than the next guy."

The Zartani nodded. "Yes. *Exactly.*"

"That's why I hate to bother you," Guinan went on. "Your time is stretched so thin already. Besides," she sighed, "with all the guests you have here, it's probably hard to remember everyone's comings and goings."

"Not at all," the manager returned.

Guinan looked surprised. "Oh?"

"In fact, I think I remember the man you're talking about. Tall, thin, bony face..."

"That's him," said Picard.

But the Zartani wasn't paying any attention to him. He was too enthralled with the captain's companion.

"Was he here recently?" she asked.

"He arrived just yesterday," said the hotel operator, "and checked out this morning."

"Really," said Guinan. "I don't suppose he mentioned where he was headed?"

The Zartani shook his head. "Not as I recall. Why are you looking for him, anyway?"

Guinan leaned a little closer to him, and when she spoke her tone was a conspiratorial one. "Believe me," she said, "you don't want to know."

Picard winced. Was that not the wrong thing to say to someone who prided himself on all he knew?

But to his surprise, the Zartani grinned and said, "I'll take your word for it."

"Wise man," Guinan told him. "I'll have to remember to send all my Zartani friends your way."

"That would be appreciated," said the Zartani.

With a parting smile, Guinan took the captain's arm and steered him away. It was only after they were back in the airlock that she let out a sigh of relief.

"You handled that rather deftly," he said.

His companion shrugged. "All I did was exercise a little patience...and listen."

"Listen?" he echoed. "I'd say you did a bit more than that. You charmed the pants off him."

"But I could only do that because I listened." She glanced at him. "That's how I was able to free you from that cell you were in—by listening."

"To my guard, you mean."

"Yes." Her eyes narrowed a bit. "And that's also how I know your name isn't Hill."

Picard felt the blood rush to his face, though it wouldn't be visible under the purple cast of his skin. He was about to tell Guinan she was mistaken, that his name really *was* Hill. Then he decided against it.

After all, she had risked her life to get him out of the detention facility, and then risked her friend's life to obtain a disguise for him. Maybe it was time he trusted her.

"You're right," he said. "My name is Picard. Jean-Luc Picard. I'm the captain of a ship called *Stargazer*."

She looked interested, but not surprised. "Really."

Then he told her about his mission, albeit in broad strokes. "So you see," he said, "why it's so urgent that I reach Demmix before he can leave Oblivion."

She looked as if she was about to say something. But before she could do so, her eyes opened wide in response to something behind him.

Picard turned and saw a security patrol passing by—three officers, all of them scanning the faces in the crowd. One of them had a padd in his hand—no doubt with a picture of Picard on its tiny screen.

They had taken it just before they placed him in his cell, hoping to match it up with a file in their database. Of course, they had been unable to do that.

But it was coming in handy now. Picard resisted an impulse to flee, knowing it would draw the security team's attention. Instead, he just stood there, letting the officers study him as they did those around him.

At first, he thought he had escaped their notice. Then one of them stared directly at him—not just for a moment, but for what seemed like an eternity. His heart started to beat harder against his ribs.

They've seen through my disguise, he told himself, and got ready to run.

But just as he was about to take off, the officer's gaze moved on to the fellow beside Picard, and kept going. The captain breathed a sigh of relief.

He felt a hand on his shoulder and knew it was Guinan's. "Looks like Dahlen did a good job," she said.

"So it does," he agreed.

Chapter Nine

OLIJ MERANT SURVEYED the crowded lobby of the Zartani hotel. Then he turned to his glinn and, in a voice intended to inspire confidence, said, "I'll be right back."

Tain, his features impassive but his eyes very much alive, said, "I have no doubt of it."

Merant wondered if his superior meant something more than he was saying. As it happened, Merant *often* found himself wondering that.

Tain was clearly more intelligent than Merant or any of the other Cardassians assigned to this mission. No one in his right mind would have questioned that.

That was why he had been promoted to the rank of glinn—because he saw angles others did not. But it seemed to Merant that Tain flaunted his superiority a little too much, in large ways as well as in small ones.

He would have said so, too, but it would surely have cost him his life. So he remained quiet and obedient, and did everything his glinn asked of him—no matter in what manner his glinn chose to ask it.

Merant turned to Beylen and Karrid, who had accompanied him and Tain to this place. Then he said, "Come on," and started in the direction of the hotel's front desk.

It was a handsome-looking place, representing the most well-to-do of the Zartani establishments Tain had identified. Its low-ceilinged lobby, which was decked out in a variety of burnished metals, had been a Dranoon captain's yacht.

The hotel proper lay beyond it, in a separate and larger but equally well appointed Enolian derelict—or so the Cardassians had been given to believe.

As Merant led Beylen and Karrid through the crowd, he knew he was in a precarious position. Having been entrusted with the task ahead of him, Merant didn't dare fail.

Not after Tain had already taken him to task for failing to snare Demmix in the plaza. Not after the glinn had reminded him of the penalty for repeated failure.

Merant almost wished that Tain hadn't named him second-in-command on their arrival here. He had been a lot happier before his promotion. He had worried less.

He was reminded of an old saying: "Those who fail the Union aren't demoted—they are *eliminated*."

But he had no intention of being eliminated.

Merant wasn't going to fail. He wasn't even going to

think about failure. He was going to find Demmix and please his glinn—no matter what it took.

With that resolve in mind, he approached the front desk, which was a converted control console of some kind. The name of the hotel, the Northern Sky, was painted in small, tasteful Zartani letters on the front edge of the console.

The Zartani manning the desk was bigger and considerably broader than most members of his species. He thrust his chin out as the Cardassians approached him, projecting what seemed to Merant to be a bit too much like defiance.

"Is there something I can do for you?" the Zartani asked, his gaze unflinching.

"There is," Merant confirmed. He took out his recording device, punched up an image of Demmix, and held it where the Zartani could study it. "Have you seen this person?"

"And if I have?"

"Then I want to know about it," the Cardassian said evenly.

The Zartani made that hideous wheezing sound that passed for laughter among his people. It grated on Merant's nerves.

"Do you now?" the hotel manager asked.

Merant could feel a gobbet of anger climb into his throat. "Is there a problem?"

"I think there is," said the Zartani. "But it's yours, not mine. You Cardassians strut around as if you own this place, but you don't. You're just another species around here."

"Really," said Merant.

Suddenly, he reached across the counter and grabbed the Zartani by the throat. The fellow tried to pry Merant's fingers loose, but he couldn't.

As the Zartani around them took notice of what was happening, they backed away. Such a courageous lot, Merant thought. Had something like this occurred on Cardassian Prime, any number of citizens would have intervened.

Unless, of course, an official of some sort was doing the strangling. That would have been a different story.

"You see what you've done?" Merant said, his face inches from the Zartani's. "You've made me angry."

He saw Beylen and Karrid spread out to make sure none of the onlookers intervened, though it was still pretty clear that no one would do so.

Normally, they would have thought twice about confronting so large a crowd. But the scrutiny of Enabran Tain could be a powerful motivator. It could make a person stronger and braver than he might have been otherwise.

And more determined. *Much* more determined.

"I…can't…can't…" the hotel operator gasped, his face darkening from lack of air.

"I think the word you're looking for is *breathe,*" said the Cardassian. "I guess that means you have a problem after all."

"Please…" the Zartani croaked.

"But with a little cooperation," said Merant, "we may solve both our problems. What do you think?"

"Y—yes..." the Zartani hissed, his eyes popping out of his head like a Rythrian's.

Merant waited just a moment longer, for emphasis. Then he released the manager from his grasp.

The fellow fell backward against the wall behind him, drawing in air in great, moaning gulps. And all the while, he stared at the Cardassian.

But not with the disrespect he had shown Merant moments earlier. There was a distinct glint of fear in his eyes now—and fear was even *better* than respect.

Tain had taught him that.

"Where were we?" asked the Cardassian. "Oh yes..." He showed the Zartani the image of Demmix again. "You were about to tell me whether you recognized this person."

The manager massaged his throat as he studied the likeness in front of him. But after a while, he shook his head. "I don't," he whispered hoarsely.

Merant scowled. "Are you certain?"

"This is a big place," the manager explained. "Dozens of Zartani come through here every day."

Merant doubted that the fellow was lying. He looked too scared, and he had nothing to gain by it.

"All right," said the Cardassian. "But if I find out your memory is faulty, you'll wish I had hung on to your throat a little longer."

Something else occurred to him.

"And if I were you," Merant added, "I wouldn't go running to the authorities. Remember, I know where to find you."

"You needn't worry," the Zartani told him.

Merant smoothed the front of his tunic. Then, with a withering glance at all the Zartani pretending not to peer in his direction, he led his underlings out of the lobby.

Nikolas hadn't eaten with anybody except Obal since Gerda Idun's departure. He just hadn't felt like it.

As difficult as it was to fend off his friend's encouragements, it would have been even more difficult to eat with people who had a less distinct idea of why the ensign was so distant.

His roommate, Paris, for example. Or Kochman. Or any of the other crewmen the ensign had been friendly with.

So when Obal wasn't available, Nikolas just ate by himself—exactly as he was doing now. He sat in a corner of the mess hall, consumed whatever he could consume in as short a time as possible, and left.

Maybe because they sensed his preference for solitude, people left him alone. Most of the time. But as Nikolas forked a piece of meatball into his mouth, he saw someone approaching him out of the corner of his eye.

Damn, he thought.

It was Hanta. And he had a hard look about him.

The Bolian walked right up to Nikolas. Then, as if he meant to confide in him, he bent over and planted his hand next to the ensign's tray.

"Can I help you?" Nikolas asked.

"I want to tell you something," said Hanta, his voice seething with barely subdued animosity.

"I'm listening, sir," the ensign said evenly.

"You took me by surprise back there in the mess hall. It won't happen again."

Nikolas turned to him. "Are you trying to scare me, sir?"

"You *should* be scared," said Hanta. "Because you're going to be decorating a bulkhead when I'm done with you."

"Permission to speak freely?"

"Permission granted."

"That's a rather hostile tone, sir. You might want to find somebody who can help you channel that anger into something positive."

Hanta's mouth twisted. "I can't think of anything more positive than shutting you up, Ensign."

"Then, if I may say so, sir, you also seem to be suffering from an acute lack of imagination."

"Suffering," said the Bolian, "is precisely what I had in mind. But it'll be yours, not mine."

"You sound pretty certain of that, sir."

"You'll get to be certain of it, too, Ensign. That is, if you've got anything resembling a brain in your head, which I'm beginning to doubt."

Nikolas managed a smile. "If I didn't know better, I'd say you were trying to get me to take a swing at you."

"Not now," said the Bolian, "and not here. But the time will come. You can rest assured of that."

"Thanks a lot," Nikolas told him blithely. "It's so hard to be certain of anything these days. At least I know there's one thing I can rely on."

Hanta didn't answer. He just glowered at him for a moment. Then the Bolian walked away, leaving his violent intentions hanging in the air behind him.

"Well," the ensign said to no one in particular, *"that* was a refreshing exchange of ideas."

Tain hadn't remained in the hotel lobby to watch Merant and the others. However, he had loitered outside the hatch that led to it and sampled the comments of the Zartani who emerged.

Unfortunately, he wasn't especially pleased with what he had overheard.

In point of fact, Tain hated the idea of delegating tasks to others. In the final analysis, he trusted no one's judgment but his own.

However, he was a glinn. He had a responsibility to separate himself from any crimes his lackeys might end up committing. If something went wrong, he was supposed to let Merant or some other underling take the blame—and they would, knowing all too well the punishment if they didn't.

They, after all, were disposable. Tain was not.

Besides, there were three hotels and two restaurants in this part of Oblivion that catered to a Zartani clientele—and with Picard on the loose, Tain couldn't have taken the time to investigate them all in order. Sending out squads was the only practical solution.

As long as they kept a low profile. As long as they were discreet about their objective.

And then, the glinn thought with a hot spurt of anger, *there is Merant....*

Tain had hoped that here, at least, the investigation would proceed to his liking. Obviously, he had been overly optimistic in that regard.

As Merant and the others emerged from the hatch, Tain studied their faces. Merant, at least, seemed oblivious of his glinn's displeasure. He looked pleased with himself, as if he had done his job and done it well.

Tain frowned. Obviously, he would have to disabuse his second-in-command of that notion.

He waited until Merant and the others had rejoined him. Then, his emotions fully contained, he said to Beylen and Karrid, "I'll see you back at our quarters."

Neither of them replied. But it seemed to Tain that they understood what was happening.

He turned to Merant next and said, "Walk with me a moment, will you?"

The other Cardassian's brow creased, but only a little. "Of course, Glinn."

Taking Merant's arm, Tain led him through the hatch and into the next hulk, which had been a Tyrheddan freighter. It now housed a series of appraisal shops, where merchants could take their recently purchased trinkets and see if they had paid a fair price for them.

"So," said the glinn, in a purposefully neutral tone of voice, "what did you learn in the Zartani hotel?"

"Unfortunately," said Merant, "nothing at all. The manager had no knowledge of the one we seek."

"You made sure of that," the glinn said. It wasn't a question. "I don't think that Zartani will be able to swallow for a while, do you?"

Merant chuckled—but there was a distinct note of nervousness in it. "Probably not."

By then, they had come to another hatch. This time, they entered the surviving portion of an Ologomwi space station, though it could hardly have been the more attractive part.

With only a row of small warehouses to commend it, it was a good deal less populated than the Tyrheddan freighter.

"Tell me," said Tain, giving nothing away, "what made you decide to grab him by the throat?"

"He was arrogant," said Merant. "I wanted to show him what I thought of his attitude."

"But all the while," Tain suggested, "you were thinking about your mission, correct? Not any personal feelings you may have entertained."

"Of course not," Merant confirmed.

They were coming to a space between two of the warehouses—an alley of sorts. And there wasn't anyone in earshot who could have overheard their conversation.

Still, what Tain had to say to Merant could be said only in complete privacy. He gestured for his second-in-command to enter the alley. Then Tain followed him.

"Is something wrong?" Merant asked.

"I need to be sure of something," Tain said. "When you choked that Zartani, were you serving Cardassia... and me?"

"Yes," Merant agreed. "Of course."

"Fully," asked Tain, "with every conceivable weapon in your arsenal?"

"I did my best," Merant said in earnest. He thrust his chin out. "And I will continue to do my best, as long as I am privileged to be in your service."

"I believe you," said Tain. But before he was finished speaking, he had pulled his disruptor out from beneath his tunic.

"What—?" Merant sputtered.

"It's unfortunate," Tain told him, "that your best has proven so woefully inadequate."

Then he depressed the trigger, skewering his fellow Cardassian on a lurid red beam.

Merant went flying into the wall behind him with bone-rattling force. Then, much more slowly, he slumped to the floor and lay still.

Tain frowned. His underling's display of violence in a crowded hotel lobby had been ill advised. The authorities would be looking for the person responsible for it, regardless of what the manager had promised Merant.

And their search would end when they found his corpse in this narrow alley.

No one fails me twice, Tain mused. Merant wasn't the first of his associates to learn that lesson, and he probably wouldn't be the last.

Putting his weapon away, the glinn walked out of the alley as if he had nothing on his mind more pressing than a pleasant meal, or perhaps a drink at one of the area's many bars.

Inside, however, he was burning.

It had nothing to do with what he had done to Merant. He wouldn't be giving that a second thought any time soon. But he was no closer than before to finding Demmix, and time was not his ally in this enterprise.

The last thing Enabran Tain wanted was to be found in a dirty alley on Cardassia Prime, the victim of a failed mission here in Oblivion.

Chapter Ten

COMMANDER STEEJ WAS SITTING in a café carved out of the bowels of an Orion slave ship, eating a plate of unfortunately overcooked Rythrian tubers, when he got the call.

Trying to contain his eagerness, he snatched his personal com device off his belt and said, "Steej here."

"This is Ardin," came the slightly tinny reply—but then, Ardin was a Zintekkan, and all his people seemed to have that vaguely metallic quality in their voices. "I'm at The Northern Sky. The manager here says he was manhandled by a Cardassian asking a lot of questions."

Steej frowned. It wasn't the report he had hoped for. "What kind of questions?"

"The Cardassian was looking for a Zartani named Demmix. He wanted to know if the fellow had taken a room at the Northern Sky."

"I see," said the Rythrian, leaning forward in his chair. "And what did the manager say?"

"He said he didn't know. That's when the Cardassian laid his hands on him, and warned him not to tell security about it if he knew what was good for him."

Steej grunted. "But he contacted us anyway."

"He was afraid of the Cardassian," said Ardin, "but he was more afraid of what might happen if he was found withholding information from us."

The Rythrian smiled to himself. It was a wise move on the part of the Zartani. When someone asked questions in Oblivion, security often wanted to know the answers as well.

"As it should be," he told Ardin.

"Shall I pursue this matter?" asked the Zintekkan. "Or keep looking for the humans?"

Steej thought about it for a moment. "The humans remain our priority. But let the others know to be on the lookout for nosy Cardassians."

"As you wish," said Ardin.

"Steej out."

As he reclipped his communications device to his belt, he pondered the incident at The Northern Sky. It wasn't unusual in a place like Oblivion for someone to demand information of someone else. After all, most of those who frequented the city were merchants, and information was perhaps the most valuable commodity of all.

But it *was* unusual for Cardassians to be involved. They always seemed to keep to themselves, conducting their business under a mantle of privacy.

The security director was intrigued. He wished he had

the time and the resources to find out who this Cardassian was, and why he had been so eager to locate a Zartani named Demmix.

And eventually, he would. But first he had to run Hill and his companion to ground.

When Picard and his companion walked into the restaurant, heads turned. *Zartani* heads, for the most part.

But then, like the hotel the captain had visited earlier, this place catered to Demmix's people. The only non-Zartani he could see were a few humans and Bolians, who had obviously developed a taste for Zartani fare.

Picard had never done that, unfortunately. He could barely tolerate the boiled-licorice smell that seemed to pervade the place.

"The owner," said Guinan, "who is also the cook, will be in the back. It's considered rude for him to serve food he hasn't taken a hand in preparing. The Zartani are funny that way."

"I know," said Picard. After all, he had learned a great deal about the Zartani through his association with Demmix.

Guinan pointed to a likely door in the rear of the dining room. "Let's go."

"By all means," he said.

He led the way, in the improbable case that they were walking into some kind of trouble. But as the door conveniently slid aside for him, he could see they were only walking into a small, well-lit kitchen.

There were three people working there, all of them

Zartani. They regarded the intruders, apprehension evident in their black, shiny eyes.

"We're looking for the owner," the captain told them.

None of them replied. But one of them glanced at another door, off to the side of the room.

"Thank you," said Picard.

"Judging from their expressions," said Guinan, "I don't think you're welcome."

Nonetheless, Picard crossed the room, with his companion right behind him. As there was a heat-sensitive plate beside the door, the captain knew it wouldn't open automatically.

With the workers looking on silently, he placed his hand on the metal plate. After a moment or two, the door whispered aside, revealing what looked like an office, with a workstation and a couple of black chairs.

The fellow sitting at the workstation didn't look up at first. He seemed to be engrossed in something on his computer screen.

He wasn't very tall, for a Zartani, and his hair had streaks of yellow mixed in with the white. More than likely, one of his ancestors had been a member of some other species.

But he had enough Zartani in him to run this eatery. That was all the captain cared about.

"If I may . . . ?" he said.

The Zartani looked up and registered surprise. "You're not Tomani," he said.

"That's true," said Picard. "Would you be the owner of this establishment?"

The Zartani tilted his head to one side—the equivalent of a nod in his culture. "I am."

"Good," said Picard. "We would like to ask your help with a matter of some importance to us."

He might as well have said that he was going to burn the place down. The Zartani's eyes grew wide with fear.

"Please," he said, "leave me alone. Haven't you done enough to us already?"

Picard didn't know what he meant. And when he exchanged glances with Guinan, it was clear that she didn't know either.

"I beg your pardon," said the captain, "but we haven't done anything at all."

The Zartani looked at them, obviously uncertain whether he should believe Picard or not. "You're not with the Cardassians?" he asked.

Picard looked at Guinan again. She shrugged.

He turned back to the restaurant owner. "We are not with *anyone*. We just want to ask you a few questions."

The Zartani stiffened again. "That's what *they* said."

"They...being the Cardassians?" Picard ventured.

The restaurant owner nodded. "A few questions, they told me. And when they didn't like my answers, they did *this*."

He held up his right hand. It was swathed in a translucent steri-seal bandage, through which Picard caught a glimpse of angry, red flesh.

"I was boiling water to make soup. They held my hand in the pot until they were certain I didn't know anything about this Zartani they were looking for."

Picard winced. "I assure you, we are completely on

our own. And we have no intention of hurting you, whether you help us or not."

The fellow looked skeptical. But then, he had been burned before—quite literally.

"How do I know you're not lying to me?" he demanded.

Guinan looked as if she wanted to intervene. No doubt she would have said something effective.

But in this case Picard didn't need any help. "You *don't* know," he said. "So if it makes you feel better, stay right where you are—and we promise to stay right where *we* are."

Out of the corner of his eye, he saw Guinan staring at him. "Took the words right out of my mouth," she muttered.

"Now," Picard continued, "you're under no obligation to help us. And if you refuse, nothing's going to happen to you. But our friend is in trouble—and if you *do* help us, it might enable us to save his life."

The Zartani frowned. "You're looking for the same person the Cardassians showed me?"

"I would imagine so," said Picard. "Lean, long hair twisted into braids, sharp features...?"

"That's the man they showed me," the restaurant owner confirmed. "But as far as I know, he hasn't been in here."

The captain was disappointed, but he believed that the Zartani was telling the truth. "Thank you," he said.

"I wish I could be of more help," said the Zartani.

So do I, Picard reflected.

But their visit hadn't been entirely unproductive.

They had learned at least one thing they didn't know before.

There was a coldblooded bunch of Cardassians looking for Demmix just as he and Guinan were—and they couldn't be allowed to find him first.

Otherwise, Demmix might receive the same sort of treatment that the restaurant owner had received. Or *worse*.

As Guinan and her companion left the Zartani restaurant, she couldn't help admiring what she had seen in Picard.

After all, he was bucking a considerable amount of adversity—the kind that might have caused a lesser individual to start showing some cracks.

It would have been different if they were making any real progress. However, they weren't much closer to finding his friend than they were when they started out.

And now their task had been made more complicated with the introduction of a mysterious pack of Cardassians—a pack that obviously had some idea of who the Zartani was and why he had come to Oblivion.

Guinan had a sneaking suspicion that it was the Cardassians who had planted the bomb in the plaza. And even these days, her suspicions were usually on the money.

In any case, *someone* had set off that bomb—someone who was willing to do more than just plunge people's hands in boiling water, horrible as that was. Some interested party, either the Cardassians or someone else, was willing to shed blood to get what they wanted.

Yet Picard didn't seem worried. In fact, he seemed

eager to take the next step in their search, regardless of where it might lead them.

He reminded her more than ever of the man she had met all those years ago in San Francisco. A man as steady as a rock, who had unhesitatingly risked his life and his mission to stay behind in that cave with her.

And the fact that he had no hair made it even easier to think of him that way.

For the first time in a long time, Guinan felt safe, protected from the forces that had tried so hard to tear her apart... and in some ways were trying *still*.

Picard didn't know that, of course. He thought he was following her, dependent on her for his salvation. But in truth, it was *she* who was following *him*.

"Mate," said Paris.

Jiterica looked surprised as she gazed at him from her seat on the other side of his table. "I beg your pardon?"

"Mate," he repeated.

Only then did he realize she could have derived a different meaning from the word than the one he had intended. Blushing fiercely, and hoping that Jiterica wasn't capable of discerning it, he pointed to the chessboard between them.

It had been a gift from his father on the occasion of his graduation from the Academy, arriving in a cargo container with the expressed sentiment that the younger Paris could learn something about tactics from it.

But Paris hadn't been thinking of tactics when he suggested that he and Jiterica play the game. He had been thinking of how it would help her develop her manual dexterity.

And, as well, he had been thinking of how it would give them something to do when they spent their off-duty time together. Somehow, the idea of just sitting and talking with her made him a little uncomfortable now.

It wasn't that way before. But since the incident in Jiterica's quarters, Paris couldn't help but look at his friend a little...differently.

"Mate?" she echoed.

Jiterica's king—a crude rendition of the traditional Terran figure carved out of Vulcan amethyst, which had retreated into a corner three moves earlier—was now effectively surrounded by Paris's amber queen and amber knight.

Jiterica studied the situation for a moment, then looked up again. "It appears you have won."

Paris nodded. "But you put up a better fight that time. *Much* better. For a moment, I thought you had me."

Behind her faceplate, her phantom brow seemed to pucker like a real one. *"Had* you?"

"Yes," he said, feeling his blush intensify again. "You were all around me and..." He stopped himself. "I mean, your *pieces* were all around me..."

Jiterica waited patiently for him to finish, apparently oblivious of Paris's discomfort.

"How about another game?" he said suddenly.

She smiled. "I would enjoy that. And this time," she added, "I will try to be aware of when you mate with me."

No, thought Paris, *not mate* with *you.*

He was about to explain Jiterica's grammatical error

when he realized that he would have to provide a literal translation of what she had said—and decided to leave the matter alone. "Good" was the response he settled for.

He forced himself not to look at his friend while they set up the board again. It gave his cheeks a chance to cool off. Finally, the pieces were all in place.

"I go first?" Jiterica asked.

Paris nodded. "Absolutely." After all, he had gone first the last time.

Jiterica moved one of her pawns forward a couple of spaces. Then she looked up at him. "You said I was permitted to do that, correct? Move two spaces, that is."

"Yes," he said, "of course."

Apparently satisfied with her opening, she sat back in her chair. As she did, the light caught her faceplate, briefly obscuring the ghostly visage behind it.

In that one moment, Jiterica's helmet looked strangely vacant—just the way Paris remembered seeing it when he barged into her quarters. That was when he looked around and came to the conclusion that she was elsewhere....

"Is everything all right?"

Jolted by Jiterica's voice, Paris blinked and realized that his friend was peering at him, her features arranged in a slightly puzzled expression.

"Uh, fine," he said.

Her puzzlement seemed to turn into concern. "Are you *certain* you're all right? You seemed...distracted."

He dismissed the idea with a wave of his hand. "Not at all. You were saying...?"

Jiterica smiled again. "I don't believe I was saying anything. I was simply waiting for you to make your move."

Paris swallowed. *Make my move...*

Again, he saw her empty suit in his mind's eye, and felt the strangely intoxicating prick of cold, cloying mist...

The ensign swore under his breath. How in the name of reason could he *not* be distracted? Being so close to Jiterica seemed to inexorably bring back the memory of how it felt to be enveloped by her... trapped in her...

It was a feeling of undeniable sensuality. Undeniable pleasure. And yes, undeniable *intimacy.*

So undeniable, in fact, that it had scared Paris right down to his soul. He could admit that now, if only to himself. That was the reason he had left Jiterica's quarters so abruptly, wasn't it? Because he was scared to death of the sensuality he felt in every alien molecule.

But it wasn't *just* sensuality—it was more than that. When he was unexpectedly immersed in Jiterica, he felt a deep and profound sense of belonging—a sense of comfort, of familiarity and undiluted acceptance.

A sense of something that felt to him a lot like love.

Not that Paris knew what love was. Not really.

After all, he had never been in love with anyone. As far as he could remember, he had never even come close. He had been too wrapped up in his studies, in his desperate attempts to meet his family's lofty expectations.

But, Paris asked himself, how could he love someone who was so vastly different from him? How could he have feelings for someone he couldn't even *hold?*

He didn't know. And yet, he had those feelings. He wasn't imagining them.

So what was the right course to take? Was he supposed to tell Jiterica how he felt and try to make a go of it with her?

No, Paris told himself. *It's too crazy.* It would never work, no matter how much he might want it to.

He had to stop it from going any further. And he had to do it now, before he did something he would ultimately regret.

"Oh no," said Paris, doing his best to look disappointed. He had never been very good at deceiving people, but he was hoping that Jiterica wouldn't notice.

She looked understandably surprised. "What is it?"

Paris sighed. "I just remembered that I'm supposed to prepare a report for Mister Simenon."

"A report?" she echoed.

"Yes, on the engine tests I ran for him this morning. I'm, er, sure you had to submit reports to him too. I mean, when you did your rotation in engineering."

"I don't recall doing so," Jiterica told him.

"Well," said Paris, "maybe he doesn't ask everyone to do them. But he won't be happy if they're late."

"I guess not," she said.

"You don't mind our cutting this short, then?"

"Not at all," said Jiterica.

"Sorry," he said—a bit lamely, he thought.

"Don't trouble yourself," she told him. "I understand."

No, he thought, *I don't think you do.* But he said, "Thanks. See you later, then?"

"Yes," said Jiterica, "later."

And she got up to leave. Paris got up as well, purely out of habit. However, he wasn't feeling particularly chivalrous after what he had just done.

He watched Jiterica turn and walk away from him. As she got closer to the doors, they opened for her, and he felt an unexpected urge to call her back—to tell her he wanted her to stay after all. But he resisted it.

Then the doors closed, and she was gone.

He took a deep breath, then expelled it. He hoped that he hadn't hurt Jiterica's feelings. After all, it wasn't her fault that he felt this way about her.

It wasn't anyone's fault. It had just *happened.*

But Paris wouldn't let it go any further. *From now on,* he told himself, *I'll have to steer clear of Jiterica.*

It wouldn't be easy. She was used to getting together with him on a regular basis. No doubt she would find it odd that he was suddenly unavailable.

And she wasn't the only one who would miss their get-togethers. *I'll miss them too,* Paris thought.

If only he hadn't walked in on her while she was out of her containment suit. If only their friendship could have remained exactly what it was, without any awkward surprises.

Unfortunately, things had changed. For both their sakes, he had to keep his distance.

It was the only way.

* * *

Picard tore off a piece of Andorian spice bread from the dark brown loaf he was sharing with Guinan, leaned back against the bulkhead of an Anjottu freighter that had been converted into a gaudy, badly illuminated marketplace, and pondered the situation in which he found himself.

In less than four hours, Demmix's flight—or rather, the flight the captain had come to *think* of as Demmix's—was scheduled to depart. And despite their having canvassed every Zartani hotel and restaurant in the area, neither he nor Guinan had the slightest idea of Demmix's whereabouts.

If they couldn't catch up with him before he got on that flight, Picard would forever lose all that Demmix knew about the Ubarrak's warships.

He was determined to keep that from happening—though he couldn't imagine how.

"There must be another way to track him down," said the captain, "something we're overlooking...."

Guinan looked at him. "He's your friend, isn't he?"

Picard met her gaze. "Yes."

"Well, you must know something more about him than the fact that he's a Zartani."

She was right, of course. Demmix had other needs besides a place to sleep and a place to eat. Picard just had to remember what they were.

He thought back to Elyrion III and its expanses of bone white prairie, baking beneath an immense, red sun. He and Demmix were among the galaxy's elite back then, individuals with something to prove both to their peers and to themselves.

And for that reason, they were very much on edge.

But Picard had learned to conceal his emotions, whereas Demmix wore his anxieties on his sleeve.

Then again, he was a nervous individual, even for a Zartani—so much so, in fact, that when he and Picard went through the mandatory, pre-race bioscans, Demmix's blood had shown trace quantities of—

Suddenly Picard had the answer he had been seeking. "That's it!" he rasped.

Guinan looked at him. *"What* is?"

He smiled triumphantly. "I think I know how we can locate Demmix."

By the time Steej reached the alley between the last two warehouses in the line, a crowd had gathered at the alley's mouth. But then, corpses were rare in Oblivion, and this one was so fresh that the blood had barely clotted.

At least, that was the report Steej had received from Yiropta, a stocky, bowlegged Enolian who was one of the security director's most trusted officers.

Yiropta hadn't discovered the body; that was the work of a passerby who had noticed something strange in the depths of the alley. But it was Yiropta who had responded to the calls for security, assessed the extent of the victim's injuries, and sealed off the alley until his superior could arrive.

He was nothing if not efficient. But then, Enolians were widely known for their efficiency.

The assembled onlookers had their backs to Steej, so none of them noticed his approach. But he wasn't about to shove his way into their midst.

"Security business," he said, wielding the phrase like a well-honed knife.

Suddenly, faces turned—all kinds of faces, representing all kinds of planetary origins. A moment later, Steej found that a path had opened for him.

Yiropta stood at the end of it. "Over here, sir," he said, jerking a stubby thumb over his shoulder.

As Steej joined him, he saw a body lying in the alleyway. As Yiropta had noted when he called in, it was a Cardassian. A big one, too.

"Any idea who he is?" he asked.

"His name is Olij Merant," said Yiropta, eyeing his superior over prominent, slitted cheekbones. "He arrived aboard a Phebracian passenger transport a few weeks ago. He was the only Cardassian aboard."

Steej knelt beside the dead man. The blackened hole in his tunic made it clear how he was murdered.

"Cut down at close range," the Enolian noted. "A robbery? Or perhaps something more personal...a dispute between friends. Or between business associates."

Steej considered all three possibilities—and rejected them. There was more to this than met the eye.

In all the time he had worked security on Oblivion, he had never seen a Cardassian involved in a crime. Now, all of a sudden, it had happened twice in a matter of just a few hours—in locations that, interestingly enough, weren't very far apart from one another.

And then there was the matter of the bomb, in a city that hadn't seen that kind of incident in years. He couldn't believe it had been a coincidence.

As the ancient Rythrians were fond of pointing out,

there *were* no coincidences in life. Clearly, there was something going on—something bigger and more complicated than Steej was initially inclined to believe.

"Place him in stasis," Steej said of the corpse. "I may want to take a closer look at him later."

"As you wish," said Yiropta.

The security director got to his feet and looked out the mouth of the alley. The faces of the crowd looked back at him—among them, perhaps, the face of the Cardassian's killer.

Or the bomber.

Or both.

He was less and less convinced that Hill was responsible for what had happened in the plaza—at least on his own. Not if this murder and the bombing were at all related.

Briefly, Steej toyed with the idea of prohibiting all Cardassians from leaving Oblivion. After all, he was already monitoring departures in his search for Hill. But the city's administrators didn't like him to impose travel restrictions, as they were bad for business.

Besides, he didn't know that the murderer was a Cardassian. It might have been the Zartani hotel manager. Or anyone else in the city, for that matter.

"Yiropta," he said, "one other thing."

"Commander?" said the Enolian.

"Send word to the other quarters that we'll need to borrow some of their officers. I want to find our friend Hill and I want to find him *now.*"

Even if he *wasn't* guilty, he might be able to shed

some light on those who were. In Steej's mind, that alone was reason to continue the search.

Yiropta nodded. "Of course, Commander."

"And the Cardassian who choked that hotel manager—I want to find him as well."

"Right away," said Yiropta.

Steej spared the Cardassian's carcass one last glance. Then he made his way through the crowd and headed back to his office, more determined than ever to get at the truth.

Chapter Eleven

"SO WHAT'S YOUR IDEA?" Guinan asked her companion.

Picard, who was sitting next to her in an obscure corner of the bazaar, had a serious fire in his eyes. But then, he seemed to believe that he had come up with the lead they needed.

"Demmix had a medication," he said. "He always carried it with him. Something for stress."

"You said he was the nervous type," Guinan recalled.

Picard nodded. "To say the least. And in a Zartani, stress is a much more serious condition than in, for instance, a human. It can even be fatal."

Guinan hadn't been aware of that. But then, she hadn't had occasion to speak with many Zartani.

"This medication," said Picard, "had to be made fresh all the time. After a couple of days, it would have lost its potency. I left orders to have some waiting for Demmix on my ship, but—"

"But thanks to that bomb," she noted, "he's not *on* your ship. And if he's feeling as stressed as we think he is—"

"He'll need to obtain some medication," said Picard, picking up the thread. "The question is—"

"Where would he find it?" Guinan smiled to herself. "I know just the place. It's not far from here, either."

"Then let's go," said her companion.

He got to his feet and extended his hand to her. As she took it, she imagined that she could feel a current of energy running through him—a current of optimism that she hadn't felt in the longest time.

Like a drowning woman, she clung to Picard for as long as she could. Then she was on her feet and she no longer had an excuse to do so.

"It's this way," she said, barely able to catch her breath. And she started in the direction of the exit.

Phigus Simenon didn't often have to discipline the crewmen who reported to him in engineering. By the time they arrived in his section, they usually knew how he felt about the importance of their individual contributions.

But every once in a while, there was an exception. In fact, he was looking at one.

What really annoyed the Gnalish was that the slacker in question wasn't a newcomer to engineering. He had worked a rotation under Simenon before—twice, actually, if memory served. And both those times, he had acquitted himself well.

But he wasn't doing that this time. For some reason, he was screwing up royally.

Waddling over to the workstation where Ensign Nikolas was sitting, Simenon peered over the man's shoulder. He could see Nikolas's monitor screen, where a brightly colored graphic was tracking the efficiency of the ship's recently upgraded power-distribution system.

"Well," said the chief engineer, "we now know ever so intimately how the EPS grid is working on Deck Six. But to get some idea of how it's working on all the other decks, you might want to call up some additional data." He tapped a key on the workstation's board. "Like so."

Nikolas kept his eyes on the screen. "Sorry, sir."

"Unless, of course," said Simenon, "there's some reason you were focusing on Deck Six to the exclusion of all the others."

"No, sir," said the ensign. "No reason."

The engineer maneuvered himself into a position between Nikolas and the screen, forcing him to meet his superior's gaze. "Then why *were* you dwelling on that particular information?"

The ensign frowned as he looked into Simenon's eyes. "I have no excuse, sir."

No excuse, the Gnalish thought. But he had been around humans long enough to know when they were suffering from lack of sleep—and Nikolas, with his dark, fleshy lower lids, was a textbook example of the problem.

"You can barely keep your eyes open," Simenon spat. "How do you expect to carry out your responsibilities in my section?"

Nikolas didn't seem nearly as offended as the engineer had intended. "All I can do is my best," he said.

Wrong answer, thought the Gnalish, a tide of anger rising in his throat—and he proceeded to address the ensign's mistake with a colorful array of his favorite words and phrases.

Though he had a feeling it wouldn't do much good.

Picard stood alongside Guinan in a small but handsomely furnished apothecary shop, and regarded the Dranoon who appeared to be the shop's proprietor.

The fellow was as every bit as broad and powerful-looking as Guinan's friend Dahlen. Being a male, however, he was understandably a bit taller. He also seemed older, judging by the thinning of his sleek, black mane.

"May I help you?" he asked in a deep, resonant voice.

Guinan placed her hands on the polished-wood counter between them. "How about a little information?"

The Dranoon laughed. "Information is a most precious commodity. It could be rather costly."

"Even for an old friend?" Picard's companion asked.

The Dranoon's expression changed to one of surprise, then disbelief. "Guinan? Is that *you?*"

She smiled. "It's me, all right."

The proprietor examined her from various angles.

"Remarkable. And if you don't mind my asking, what occasioned this rather ill-advised change of appearance?"

"Believe me," she said, "you don't want to know. Just tell me one thing—did a Zartani come in here recently to buy a bottle of Geyanna extract?"

The Dranoon nodded his squarish head. "Yes. Just this morning, actually. He purchased a small supply, though he could have saved on a larger one." His brow knit. "Why do you ask?"

"You don't want to know that either," said Guinan.

The Dranoon considered the remark for what seemed like a long time. Finally, he expelled a husky sigh and said, "All right. If you say so."

Picard felt grateful. As Guinan had pointed out, it would be better for the Dranoon if he didn't have any knowledge of what they were up to. But it was even more important to the captain and his companion.

Just then, he caught a glimpse of a blue-and-black uniform through the shop's transparent display window. "Guinan," he whispered urgently.

She had noticed it too, it seemed. But if she had even considered asking her friend to conceal them, the option quickly became unavailable. Before either Guinan or Picard could make a move, a Tyrheddan security officer walked through the wide-open doorway of the apothecary shop.

He wasn't alone, either. The captain saw several of the officer's colleagues outside, waiting for him.

If the Dranoon was nervous, he didn't show it. "Good day, Lieutenant. How can I help you?"

The security officer didn't respond with the same warmth, scanning the shop with his single cyclopean eye. "We're looking for a couple of humans." He handed the proprietor a padd. "Have you seen them?"

The Dranoon studied the image on the padd's tiny screen. Picard saw his face there, right beside Guinan's. But thanks to Dahlen, they didn't look like that anymore.

"Can't say I have," the Dranoon said. He handed the padd back to the officer. "What did they do?"

Muscles twitched around the officer's eye. "Never mind that. Just watch for them. If you catch sight of them, report it immediately."

"I will," the Dranoon promised him.

The officer stared at him for a full second, as if to impress the store owner with the seriousness of the matter. Then he turned to Picard and Guinan.

For a moment, he seemed to see that there was something odd about them. Something familiar, even. The captain felt a drop of perspiration trickle down the back of his neck.

Then the officer said, "That goes for you too."

Picard nodded. "Of course."

"No problem," Guinan assured him.

With a last glance at the Dranoon, the officer left the shop. It wasn't until after he and his men were all out of sight that Picard felt a wave of relief.

Turning to Guinan's friend, he said, "Thank you."

"For what?" the Dranoon asked. "I answered honestly. I *haven't* seen those people." He glanced at Guinan in a conspiratorial way. "Lately, at least."

"Before we were interrupted," said Picard's companion, "we were talking about a Zartani. I don't suppose he made mention of where he was staying?"

The Dranoon's features squeezed together as he thought about it. "I don't believe so," he said at last.

Picard's hopes fell.

"Do you remember him saying anything about where he was headed?" Guinan asked.

Her friend thought some more—and a light went on in his round, dark eyes. "As I was preparing the extract, he asked about a footwear vendor. He said his heel hurt him."

The captain nodded. "That sounds right." The same slender leg and foot bones that made Demmix's people such splendid runners also made them vulnerable to injury.

"Where did you send him?" Guinan asked.

"There's a place two hulls down," said the Dranoon, "in *that* direction." And he pointed with a thick green finger.

Picard followed the gesture to a distant hatch. Then he turned to his companion. "Do you know of any Zartani accommodations in that direction?"

Guinan shook her head. "No. There are a couple of hotels that way, but neither of them is designed to accommodate Zartani."

The captain frowned. Would Demmix have risked staying in a non-Zartani sleeping environment in order to avoid detection until he left Oblivion? It might explain why they were having such a difficult time finding him.

"Thanks," Guinan told the owner of the apothecary shop. "I guess I owe you one."

He smiled paternally. "You owe me *more* than one, but you can take your time paying me back." Then, to Picard, he said, "I hope you find the fellow you're looking for."

"So do I," said the captain.

Enabran Tain eyed the manager of the Singing Waters across the top of the fellow's stained metal desk.

The glinn declined to guess what kinds of stains they were, considering the fact that this had once been the galley of a Klingon transport, and Klingons were known to eat their food freshly slaughtered.

Like The Heavenly Meadow, the Singing Waters was a hotel that catered to Zartani. Tain hoped to have better luck there than in the other places he had visited.

"I'm looking for someone," he said.

The manager's expression indicated that he didn't often see Cardassians. But then, Tain wouldn't have expected him to.

"Maybe you've seen him," he added, handing over a palm-sized recorder with Demmix's likeness on it.

The Zartani studied it for a moment. Then he returned the recorder. "He doesn't look familiar."

"You're certain?" Tain asked.

"Quite certain," the Zartani told him. "I have no reason to conceal anything from you."

Tain nodded. "I'm glad to hear that."

His eyes were drawn to the wall behind the Zartani.

There was a shelf there supporting a holoprojector—not the latest kind, but one that seemed to work pretty well nonetheless.

It depicted the hotel manager along with three others. One was a female, obviously his mate. The other two were his offspring, both males.

They seemed to be enjoying each other's company. It was a nice scene, a family scene.

Touching, thought Tain.

He held out the recorder again. "So you're certain you haven't seen this man?"

The Zartani nodded. "Yes."

Tain pointed to the hologram. "Lovely family."

The Zartani didn't turn around to look at it. However, the furrow in his brow indicated that he knew what the Cardassian was referring to.

"Thank you," he said a little shakily.

"You must be very attached to them," Tain observed.

The Zartani swallowed hard and visibly. "Of course."

"Do they live in Oblivion?" Tain asked.

He didn't get an answer.

"I'll bet they do," said Tain. "A family man like you wouldn't want to be separated from his wife and children."

The furrow in the Zartani's brow grew deeper.

"It would be a pity," the Cardassian continued matter-of-factly, "if anything happened to them."

The Zartani's eyes widened. "Please," he said, his voice taut with apprehension, "it's as I told you—I don't know anything about the man you're looking for."

Tain studied the fellow's face for a moment. As far as he could tell, the Zartani was telling the truth.

"That's unfortunate," he said reasonably. "I guess I'll have to look elsewhere."

The manager appeared to relax a bit.

Tain eyed him a little longer. Then he left, his men following in his wake.

Time is running out, he told himself. He had to find Demmix soon, or risk losing him to the human.

And Tain wasn't a very good loser.

Chapter Twelve

IT'S TIME, Ulelo thought.

Time to report to the bridge, as he did at least once a day, and take over the communications panel from Paxton or one of the other com officers. Time to do his work until he was sure that no one was looking.

And, once he felt sure he was unobserved, time for him to betray the captain and crew of the *Stargazer.*

At least, that was the way it had gone for the last several weeks, as Ulelo transmitted to his comrades whatever data he thought they might find useful.

"My stop," said Emily Bender.

Ulelo halted in his tracks. He was so deep in thought, he had missed the small sign identifying the double set of doors as the entrance to the science section.

"Sorry," he said.

"Man," said Emily Bender, "you seem like you're in another world today."

"Do I?" asked Ulelo.

"Uh-huh." Emily Bender smiled. "Try not to accidentally open a channel to Romulus, all right?"

He managed to return her smile. "Don't worry."

She looked into his eyes. "What's on your mind, anyway?"

"Nothing, really," said Ulelo. "I just didn't sleep very well last night."

It was a lie, of course. He had experienced a peaceful, uninterrupted sleep, as always.

But Emily Bender didn't question the veracity of his answer. She just nodded.

"I should go," said the com officer.

"Of course," Emily Bender responded. "Thanks for walking me to work. And—"

"Yes?" he said.

"I'm glad we're friends."

He hadn't expected her to say that. "Er...me, too."

It was the truth. One of the few he had uttered since he joined the crew, in fact.

Emily Bender shrugged. "I know I originally wanted us to be more than that, but I'm happy with the way it worked out." She paused. "I just wanted to say that."

Ulelo nodded. "I'm happy, too."

Then his friend did something *really* unexpected. She got up on her toes and kissed him on the cheek.

He didn't know what to say. Fortunately, Emily Bender filled the silence after a moment.

"Get going," she said. "I don't want to make you

late." Then she went through the sliding doors and left him standing there.

Ulelo looked down the corridor to the turbolift that would take him up to the bridge. It was empty.

And even if it hadn't been, his crewmates were unaware of his secret transmissions. They knew the com officer as a man they passed in the hallways or worked alongside or with whom they attended holographic concerts.

But no one knew him for what he really was.

So there was nothing to stop Ulelo from relieving Lieutenant Paxton on the bridge, sitting down at the communications station, and doing what he had intended to do.

Nothing except himself.

But at the moment, it seemed, that was enough.

Ulelo couldn't bring himself to transmit another packet of strategically important information. He just didn't have the stomach to go on betraying his friends.

Especially Emily Bender.

He tried to imagine the look on her face if he was caught and his activities exposed. He tried to imagine the shock, the disappointment.

What would Emily Bender say to him if he were apprehended? Ulelo couldn't imagine. Or maybe he just didn't want to.

She had opened her heart to him. She had given him things he didn't think he had ever had before—things like friendship and camaraderie, and trust. He couldn't repay her by continuing with his mission.

But what about the comrades to whom Ulelo had been transmitting—the ones who sent him here in the first place? Didn't he owe them his allegiance as well?

It was a hard choice to make. He wished he could recall more, so he could know if he had made such a decision before, and what the outcome had been.

But he didn't remember. His past was a haze, punctuated only occasionally with points of clarity.

In the absence of experience, Ulelo had to go with his feelings. He had to go with his heart. And his heart was telling him to think of Emily Bender.

With that in mind, he headed for the bridge. But this time, he wasn't going to transmit any secrets. He was just going to man the communications panel.

And ignore the reason he was here.

As Enabran Tain led his men past an exotic pet shop, deep in the hold of an old Jadaral grain ship, he found himself pausing to examine the specimens in the shop's display window.

A tiny Klingon *targ,* its jaws slavering, probably less than a week old but already as vicious as it would be as an adult. A Regulan eel bird, dark and rubbery-looking except for its curious, diamondlike eyes. A Kavarian tiger bat hanging upside down from a metal bar in its cage, its wildly striped wings wrapped about it like a second skin.

As he watched, the tiger bat shuddered, seemingly caught in the throes of a disturbing dream. The Cardassian couldn't help smiling to himself.

He had always been intrigued by the behavior of subsentient species. As a boy, he had gone out of his way to find and study them in the sparsely forested hills about his home.

Tain recalled an instance when he was not more than nine years old. One of his friends caught an *idaja*—a delicate, insectlike life form with long, graceful legs and wings that changed color in the sunlight.

His friend decided it would be fun for him to pluck the *idaja*'s wings off. Tain didn't like the idea. He told his friend to hand the *idaja* over.

When his friend refused, Tain beat him bloody, nearly blinding him in one eye. By that time, the *idaja* had fallen from his friend's hand onto a patch of bare, dry ground.

With the utmost care, Tain picked the creature up and examined it in the brassy sunlight. Its wings fluttered, changing from green to blue and then to yellow.

Remarkable, he had thought.

Then he caught one of the *idaja*'s wings between his thumb and his forefinger, and pulled just hard enough to tear it loose—exactly as his friend had intended to.

But even then, Tain had a sense that life's privileges were the province of the strong. That was why he had never allowed himself to become weak.

Tapping on the display window with his forefinger, he angered the *targ* and made it leap repeatedly in his direction. He would have liked to stay and watch the beast's frustration, but he had a Zartani to find.

Abruptly, the Cardassian felt the buzzing of his com device. Removing it from his tunic, he spoke into its triangular input grate. "Tain here."

"This is Varitis, Glinn."

Tain's eyes narrowed. He had posted Varitis at one of the city's docking ports. "I'm listening."

"It appears that we're not the only ones looking for the Zartani. Rumor has it that a couple of Cataxxans are looking for him too."

"Cataxxans?" said Tain. "And you say there were a couple of them? As in *two?*"

"That's correct, Glinn. One male and one female."

Tain pressed his knuckle into his lips. His underlings had yet to find any sign of the two humans. But now, there were a couple of Cataxxans searching for Demmix.

Coincidence? He didn't think so.

After all, how much would it take to make a human resemble a Cataxxan? Not much at all. A little hair removal, a little purple dye, and the transformation would be complete—at least to the casual observer.

"Stay alert for any further word on these Cataxxans," Tain said. "And tell the others to stay alert as well."

"Of course, Glinn," said Varitis.

"Tain out."

Slipping his com device back into his tunic, he made a mental note to give Varitis the position left vacant by Merant as soon as this mission was over.

And why not? Varitis had given the glinn an important second option. Before, he had no choice but to find Demmix. Now, if his instincts were correct, he could simply find Picard—and let *him* lead the way to Demmix.

Once more, he tapped on the window and watched the *targ* fly into a fury. Then he gestured to Beylen and Karrid, and led the way to yet another Zartani hotel.

* * *

152

Steej was back in his office, scrolling through a list of the last hour's worth of field reports, when he received a call on his com device.

"Steej here," he said.

"It's Ardin. I'm at the Coastal Breezes—and we've got another report about Cardassians asking questions. Except this time, there was only one of them."

"Was he asking about the Zartani?"

"According to the proprietor."

Steej sat back in his chair. Obviously, this Demmix was a very important fellow to *someone.*

Had he been important to the Cardassian they found in the alley? And had that fact somehow contributed to the Cardassian's bloody demise?

It certainly seemed likely.

"That's not all," said Ardin. "There are a couple of Cataxxans asking questions too now."

Steej made a face. "Cataxxans?" They were the most upright species he knew—hardly the sort to be engaged in anything shady.

"I know, sir. It seems unusual. But apparently, they showed up at the Coastal Breezes after the Cardassian did."

"And?" said Steej.

"And they asked questions about Demmix as well. But without any threat of violence."

The Rythrian nodded to himself. *An important fellow* indeed.

"I'm dispatching additional personnel to your sector," he told Ardin. "Have them go around to all the Zartani hotels in the area and warn the proprietors about these

Cardassians—and the Cataxxans too, while you're at it. Tell them we need to know immediately about any visits they get."

"Yes, sir," came the response. "Ardin out."

Steej frowned as he put his com device away. Cataxxans, eh? Who else was going to turn up in the course of his investigation? Some Gorn? A few Vulcans, perhaps?

Whatever was going on, it was bigger than he had ever imagined. But then, he consoled himself, it would be that much more satisfying when he got to the bottom of it.

For him, at least. For those who had committed crimes in his jurisdiction, it would anything *but* satisfying.

Commander Wu had barely sat down to eat a quick plate of stir-fried vegetables when she heard someone call her name.

Looking up, she saw Pierzynski, a big, blond security officer, standing there with a tray full of something hot and steaming.

"Mind if I sit down?" he asked.

Wu indicated the chair opposite hers. "Please do."

"Thanks," said Pierzynski.

He put his food down and folded himself into the chair. Then he glanced at the second officer's tray.

"Not very hungry?" he asked.

"Not especially," she replied. "But then, I've never been a very big eater."

The security officer nodded. "I've always been the opposite. After I'm done with this plate, I'll probably go back and get another one. Fast metabolism, I guess."

Wu smiled. "So it would seem."

For all his vaunted appetite, Pierzynski didn't seem especially interested in his food. "Have we heard anything from the captain?" he asked.

It seemed to be the question on everyone's mind. But then, given Picard's popularity, it would have been surprising if it had been otherwise.

Wu could only imagine the crew's response if they knew the captain hadn't reported in yet, many hours after his intended rendezvous.

She shook her head. "Not yet. But we believe that we'll hear something soon."

Pierzynski nodded. "Good."

And he dug into his meal. But from Wu's point of view, the security officer still looked like a man with something on his mind. It occurred to her that his request to sit with her might not have been an entirely casual one.

Finally, he sat back and wiped his mouth. Then, in what seemed like an intentionally offhand manner, he said, "Actually, there's something I'd like to ask you about."

Ah-hah, Wu thought. "And what would that be?"

Pierzynski took a deep breath, then said, "As you know, I've been a security officer for three years now—two on the *Lantree* and one on the *Reliant*."

"Yes," she said, "I'm aware of that." She made a point of knowing her crew's personnel files backward and forward.

Pierzynski went on. "When we left spacedock, I was Lieutenant Ang's right-hand man. At least, that's how it seemed to me."

Wu saw where he was going. "However, the captain made Mister Joseph acting security chief when Lieutenant Ang left the ship."

Pierzynski nodded. "I like Lieutenant Joseph. I think he's doing a great job. And even if he weren't, I wouldn't try to stab him in the back or anything."

Just then, the second officer saw Ensign Jiterica enter the mess hall. Passing the food slot, she found a table and sat down by herself.

Of course, the Nizhrak didn't eat food. Lacking the organs typical of a humanoid digestive system, she couldn't have consumed anything even if she had wanted to.

As Wu watched, the ensign started working on a personal display device, using the bulky fingers of her containment suit with a dexterity she couldn't have exhibited when she first came aboard the *Stargazer.* No doubt, she was continuing some bit of work she had begun during her last shift in the science section.

Of course, seeing Jiterica with that device in hand was nothing new. She brought it to the mess hall every day, just as soon as she was relieved of her post.

The second officer smiled, knowing it was she who originally suggested that the ensign bring the device with her to the mess hall. Indeed, it was she who suggested that Jiterica come to the mess hall in the first place.

It had started out as a personal invitation—a way for Wu and Jiterica to get to know each other better, at least on the face of it. But really, it was an attempt to introduce the ensign to the social life of the crew.

It turned out to be a disaster—at least partly because

of the design of the mess-hall chairs. Built for humanoids, they had prevented Jiterica from sitting comfortably and added to her self-consciousness instead of relieving it.

A *huge* disaster, Wu amended.

But she had still believed in the need for the ensign to be in the mess hall, so she placed a more containment-suit-friendly chair in the room. That helped.

And after Jiterica's work on the rescue of the *Belladonna*, she had gotten more positive attention from her colleagues in the science section. That helped as well.

Pretty soon, the Nizhrak had become a fixture in the mess hall—usually one of several science-section personnel in the corner farthest from the replicator station.

Unfortunately, none of her colleagues from the science section seemed to be around at the moment. The only crewmen in the place were from the security and engineering sections, and Jiterica didn't know them quite as well.

Which, Wu concluded, was why the ensign was sitting all by herself.

"—and if you think Lieutenant Joseph is better officer material than I am," said Pierzynski, "and you want to make him the permanent chief of security, I can live with that. But at this point, I don't know what you, the captain, or Commander Ben Zoma have in mind for him.

"And if you bring in somebody else and make Mister Joseph just a regular officer again, that makes me number three in the section. And under those circumstances, I think I may be better off asking for a transfer."

Wu wanted to give Pierzynski her undivided attention. But she couldn't help thinking about Jiterica.

The ensign didn't *appear* to have a problem with the solitude—but Wu did. The last thing she wanted was for the Nizhrak to start feeling lonely again, especially after she had been making such excellent progress.

"So," said Pierzynski, "I'd just like to know where I stand."

Wu nodded. "I understand your concerns. Unfortunately, I don't know what the captain has in mind at this point."

The security officer sighed.

"On the other hand," the second officer continued, "I can tell you that we're all very pleased with your work, and would like you to remain on the *Stargazer*. And if you should decide to ask for a transfer, we will do everything we can to get you the kind of posting you deserve."

That seemed to make Pierzynski feel a little better. "Thanks," he said.

They spoke a little longer. Then the security officer picked up his tray and left Wu sitting there—wondering what she should do about Jiterica.

The ensign was still sitting alone, still working on her padd. And her solitude still bothered the second officer.

Wu considered the idea of rectifying the problem herself, by picking up her tray and sitting down next to Jiterica. However, she was due back on the bridge and she couldn't have stayed very long.

She was still considering the matter when Ensign

Paris walked in—and gave Wu reason to feel relieved. She didn't need to feel bad anymore. Help had arrived.

Of everyone on board the *Stargazer,* Cole Paris was probably the individual closest to Jiterica. Nor was it a surprise to Wu that that should be the case.

Paris had worked with Jiterica on the rescue of the *Belladonna,* which was caught in the grip of a deadly space anomaly. When they returned from their mission, there was a bond between them—or at least the beginnings of a bond. The second officer had seen it in their faces, and the realization had pleased her no end.

After all, Jiterica hadn't made any friends yet at that point, and she had needed one desperately. The rescue mission had presented her with at least the possibility that she would find friendship on board the *Stargazer.*

And once the ensign got a glimpse of that possibility, she was able to interact with her colleagues in the science section on an entirely different footing. She was able to make friends of them as well.

Ironically, Wu recalled, Paris didn't end up seeing Jiterica for a while afterward, since they were on unavoidably different schedules. But when he finally *did* see her, they began spending much of their free time together.

Wu glanced at Jiterica to see her reaction to Paris's appearance. Indeed, the ensign seemed pleased by the prospect of having her friend join her, a ghostly smile growing behind her faceplate.

Paris glanced in Jiterica's direction, then headed for the food slot. Naturally, Wu expected him to join the Nizhrak as soon as he filled his tray.

But he didn't. In fact, he walked over to the opposite side of the room, where no one else was sitting, and sat down at a table all by himself.

Strange, thought Wu.

She didn't know what to make of it. And a glance at Jiterica told her the ensign didn't know what to think either.

One thing was for sure—the second officer was going to have a talk with Ensign Paris.

Enabran Tain left the last Zartani hotel on his itinerary with an irresistible desire to strangle someone.

It wasn't that he hadn't finally picked up a lead with regard to Demmix's whereabouts. It was that the lead didn't appear to *lead* anywhere.

Granted, the glinn now knew where Demmix had slept prior to the plaza bombing—right there in The Heavenly Meadow. However, he still didn't know where the Zartani was headed when he left the hotel. And the manager there, for all the apparent effectiveness of Tain's increasingly open threats, seemed incapable of producing that information.

Time was going by and he had snared neither Demmix nor Picard in his web. He didn't like that. He didn't like it at all.

Just then, he felt the buzzing of his com device. Taking it out, he snarled, "Tain."

"It's Varitis, Glinn."

"I want good news," Tain snapped.

"I have some," Varitis told him with undisguised eagerness. "I have spotted the two Cataxxans."

Now we're getting somewhere, Tain told himself. "Where are they?"

His underling told him.

"I'm on my way," said Tain.

Gesturing for Beylen and Karrid to follow him, he headed for the location Varitis had given him—hoping their hunt would soon be over.

Chapter Thirteen

PICARD LOOKED AT the black-and-white-striped Dedderac who operated the footwear emporium on the transfer deck of an Athabascid deuterium tanker.

"A Zartani?" he echoed.

"Yes," said Guinan.

"I just came in a few minutes ago," said the Dedderac. "But if you like, I can ask someone."

"By all means," said Picard.

The Dedderac called over one of his employees, a human with a shock of blond hair and a stubbly brush of beard on his chin. "Braddock," he said, "did you wait on a Zartani today?"

The fellow nodded. "Just a few hours ago. Sold him a pair of special-supports." He glanced at Picard. "He said his feet hurt so much he couldn't stand it another second."

"Did he happen to mention where he was staying?"

asked the captain, repeating what he and his companion had asked so often that day already.

"Not exactly," said Braddock.

"Not exactly?" Guinan echoed.

"He asked directions to the Emperor's Eye. That's a hotel not too far from here. But he was a Zartani, so I didn't think he was actually going to stay there."

Picard exchanged looks with his companion. "Do you know where the Emperor's Eye is?" he asked.

Guinan nodded. "As our friend here said, it's not far. All we have to do is—"

Suddenly, she fell silent. Her eyes, it seemed, were fixed on something behind the captain.

He turned to see what might have drawn her attention, but all he saw was a multilevel display full of children's footwear—and a colored ball lit from within, a child's toy used to add interest to the display.

That was it. But for some reason, Picard's companion couldn't seem to take her eyes off it.

"Guinan?" he said.

It was then that the captain realized she was weeping. The notion came as a shock to him. To that point, he had barely seen her display any emotion at all.

"Are you all right?" he asked her.

Guinan nodded, then turned to him—with what seemed like a certain amount of effort. "Fine."

"You're sure?"

"I said I was fine," she told him.

Picard felt the need to probe deeper, but forced himself to respect the woman's privacy. If she wanted to tell him what had happened, she would do so. And if she didn't...

He put his hand on her arm. "You were telling me how to get to the Emperor's Eye...?"

"Right," she said. She took a deep breath, her nostrils flaring. "No problem."

Picard thanked the store manager and the human called Braddock. Then, keeping a close, concerned eye on Guinan, he followed her out into the shopping area's main thoroughfare.

Guinan brushed away a lingering tear as she led Picard in the direction of the Emperor's Eye.

Odd, she thought, *the way things work out.* She had been on her guard for so long, avoiding anything that might have reawakened the feelings she had worked to submerge.

And in the end, what had brought those feelings rushing back like a river in full flood? A child's toy. A simple Tellati child's toy.

But it was exactly the color of sunset in a place Guinan had never really visited—at least not in the sense one *usually* visited places. She knew that didn't make sense, but the entire experience was still such a confusion to her, defying her attempts to attach words to it.

It had happened when she was on a ship called the *Lakul*—one of two ungainly transport vessels crawling through the vault of space, each one packed to the bulkheads with her people. But it wasn't by choice that any of them had come that way.

They were refugees, the last of their kind, stripped of everything and everyone they had held dear by a half-living blight called the Borg.

For months, Guinan and the remnants of her once-numerous species had gone from vessel to vessel, all the while mourning their planet, their loved ones, and the lives they had left behind. Their destination? A world called Earth at the heart of the Federation.

Guinan had been on Earth before, hundreds of years earlier. But since her last visit, the place had changed quite a bit—or so she had heard. It was no longer a world of soot-belching chimneys and hard-grinding engines. It had become a calmer and gentler world, regaining much of its pristine splendor.

The El-Aurians—Guinan's people—had been told they could build new lives there on Earth. And they clung fiercely to that hope, for it was all they had left.

Then they ran into the Nexus—a twisting, blinding-bright ribbon of anomalous energies floating imperiously through otherwise empty space.

How she wished they had taken some other route, or traveled at a different speed, and thereby avoided even seeing the thing. But Fate placed it directly in their path.

At first, their captain hadn't thought much of the phenomenon. He considered it a curiosity, nothing more. But he changed his mind when the *Lakul* began to shear toward it, caught in its wildly powerful gravimetric distortion field.

Their sister ship, the *Robert Fox*, tried to assist the *Lakul*. But in extending that assistance, she was snared by the phenomenon as well.

When the *Lakul*'s captain realized what kind of straits they were in, he sent out a distress call. Later, they would find out that it was received by the *Enterprise*, an

Excelsior-class starship just out of space dock, not far from Earth.

But after a while, neither Guinan nor her fellow refugees were concerned with the possibility of being rescued. In fact, it was the furthest thing from their minds.

Because by then, the Nexus had claimed them.

Guinan couldn't have said how long she was in that odd, timeless place. Just a few hours, apparently, judging by the timing of the distress call and the *Enterprise*'s arrival. But it seemed like a lot more—and also, a lot less.

Then again, how does one measure bliss? How does one quantify complete and utter peace?

Guinan's family was there, or at least she thought it was—and her friends were there as well. All the people she thought she had lost forever to the metal appendages of the Borg...they had miraculously been returned to her.

Even Jevi.

The daughter who, of all Guinan's daughters, was most like her. The child she had borne when all the others were grown and gone.

Jevi was there in the Nexus, in all her beauty and innocence, in all her brilliance and simplicity. She was there for Guinan to see and hold and hear and smell, every bit as sweet and solid and full of giggles as the day the Borg had taken her.

Guinan knew in her heart that Jevi wasn't real. She couldn't be. But Guinan didn't care in the least. She was home again. She was free from sadness and stuggle. She was a mother, loved and loving, cradling her baby in her arms.

And she never, ever wanted to leave.

In time, however, the *Enterprise* arrived. Her captain saw that both the *Lakul* and her sister ship were gradually coming apart, savaged by the terrible forces exerted by the Nexus.

Tragically, he was too late to save the *Robert Fox*. As he and his bridge officers watched in horror, the Nexus crushed the transport's hull—killing all of the two hundred and seventy-five El-Aurians aboard.

But the *Lakul* was a little sturdier—or maybe just a little luckier. She wouldn't yield to the Nexus until forty-seven of her passengers had been beamed from her buckling decks to the safety of the *Enterprise*'s sickbay.

The starship herself suffered only one casualty—a retired Starfleet captain named Kirk, who was only supposed to have been a guest on the vessel. He perished helping the *Enterprise* free herself from the phenomenon.

Guinan was one of the forty-seven El-Aurians who came through the ordeal alive—twice a survivor. But at first, when she was milling about in the *Enterprise*'s sickbay, she wished that hadn't been the case.

That's how much it hurt to have the joy and contentment of the Nexus ripped from her without warning. That's how much it tore her up to lose Jevi and the others a second time.

When she left that junction of infinite possibilities, it felt as if she had abandoned a part of herself. And in her grief, she couldn't help feeling that it was by far the *best* part.

The *Enterprise* took Guinan the rest of the way to

Earth, but she wasn't aware of the voyage. She was too disoriented, too much in shock.

The other El-Aurians were the same way. They wandered from place to place without purpose, babbling about colors no one had ever heard of and the sound of time—or so Guinan was told in years to come.

Eventually, with the help of Federation counselors on Earth, she and all the other survivors of the *Lakul* regained their equilibrium. They became capable of functioning and fending for themselves again.

It wasn't easy. For years, Guinan barely spoke, barely raised her eyes to look into someone else's.

But little by little, she reclaimed herself. She rediscovered the points of contact between herself and the real world. With patience and slow, painstaking effort, she rebuilt the Guinan she had known.

The hardest part was accepting that she would never again feel what she had felt in the Nexus, that she would never again know that unmitigated joy and contentment.

But somehow she did it. She moved on.

Then, a little less than a year ago, Guinan had felt the Nexus's siren call again. The phenomenon was passing through the Alpha Quadrant on its thirty-nine-year loop, tugging on the invisible bonds in which it had bound her.

She could see it from the observation ports of a half-dozen different hulks—a majestic ribbon of fiery energies, undulating through space less than three thousand kilometers from Oblivion. It was almost as if it had known where to find her.

The sight of it reopened all her wounds, reminding her of the terrible depth and breadth of her loss. And she was tempted—so terribly tempted—by the joy she had known in the Nexus's embrace.

The effort to resist its lure left Guinan weak, withdrawn, dispirited—hardly any better off than when the *Enterprise* had rescued her. And when the Nexus went away again, taking that sweet, undefinable portion of her with it, her outlook didn't improve.

If anything, it got worse.

Once again, Guinan had a hard, steep road ahead of her. But this time, she didn't have any Federation counselors to give her a hand. All she had was herself, and the few good friends she had made in Oblivion.

They tried to bring her out of her malaise, Dahlen and the others...they tried as hard as she could ever have expected of them.

But she couldn't feel. She couldn't even contemplate the possibility of feeling. All she could do was move from day to day and darkness to darkness, surviving but not really living—not anymore, not the way she used to before the Nexus laid its claim to her.

And that was the state Guinan had been in when Picard sat down next to her at the bar—without even knowing who she was, as if Fate herself had taken a hand again.

And he had done for her what no one else could, because he was different from anyone else. He was the man from the future. He was the man from her past.

He was her salvation.

Guinan resisted the urge to look back at the Tellati ball. How strange, she thought again, that a child's toy should evoke such joy and misery in her. Such memories...

Not so long ago, they would have buried her beneath

the weight of longing and despair. But not with Picard at her side. With him there, she could—and would—go on.

Tain found Varitis right where he said he would be—in front of a shadowy Tyrheddan restaurant in the midst of a large, bustling shopping area.

The glinn had only one question when he arrived at Varitis's side: "Where?"

His underling lifted his chin to point across the shopping area's main thoroughfare. "There, Glinn. In that footwear shop across the way."

Tain eyed the place. It had display windows, but he couldn't see anyone inside. "You're sure they're in there?"

"Yes, Glinn."

"For how long now?"

"Several minutes," said Varitis.

Several minutes is a long time, Tain reflected. Had the visit been an unproductive one, the Cataxxans would likely have emerged a good deal sooner.

Unless they really went in to buy footwear, he thought. The glinn might have laughed if he hadn't been so intent on snaring his quarry.

"Your orders?" asked Varitis.

"Spread out," said Tain, "so it's not quite so obvious that we're surveilling the place. But be alert for the moment when the Cataxxans leave. That's when we'll—"

Before he could finish, he saw two figures emerge from the footwear shop. A pair of Cataxxans—a male and a female, just as Varitis had said.

At least, they *appeared* to be Cataxxans. But no one knew better than Tain, who had studied the arts of espionage back on Cardassia Prime, how deceiving an appearance could be.

Fortunately, he had a way to examine the Cataxxans that went deeper than how they looked. Reaching into his tunic, he found it—a flat device about the size of his palm, which he extracted and cupped in his hand. When he pressed a stud on its side, a tiny readout screen lit up.

The device was a sensor, designed to detect enemy life signs in combat situations. Tain had never been in combat but he carried it anyway, as it was useful in his line of work to know one's friend from one's foe.

Pointing the sensor at the Cataxxans, he studied the screen. For a moment or two, what he saw was confused by the presence of passersby. Then the thoroughfare cleared and he was able to take an unobstructed reading.

It gave the Cardassian reason to applaud his instincts.

One of the Cataxxans was actually a human—Picard, no doubt, with a skillfully altered appearance. The other was a member of a species Tain's device couldn't readily identify.

But, clearly, neither of them was Cataxxan.

"Stay here," the glinn told Varitis. "Ask the store owner about his conversation with those two."

Varitis nodded. "Certainly, Glinn."

In the meantime, Tain and his other two underlings would follow Picard and his companion at a distance. And with a little luck, they would discover that the human was further along in the search for Demmix than they were.

Tain smiled to himself. Maybe the "Cataxxans" had obtained the last bit of information they needed in that footwear shop and were going to meet Demmix at that very moment. Wouldn't that be a pleasant development?

For him, at least. For everyone else involved, it could turn out most *un*pleasant.

Tain was still waiting for the right moment to start following Picard and his companion when he saw something that made his gut clench. It wasn't much—just a nuance of movement in the crowd that someone else would likely have missed.

It forced a curse from him.

"Glinn?" one of his men said.

"Quiet!" he snapped.

There—he saw it again. Tain was dead certain of it now.

The place was crawling with plainclothes security personnel. And they were homing in on Picard and his companion as if they were aware of the fugitives' true identities.

Tain shook his head in disgust. *This is bad,* he thought. *This is* very *bad.*

If the authorities nabbed Picard and the female, they wouldn't be able to lead the Cardassians to Demmix. All Tain's work to this point would be for nothing.

But what could he do about it? Set up a diversion so the captain could escape?

Too risky, the glinn decided. And besides, even if Picard did elude security, there was no guarantee that Tain would find him again before he located Demmix.

The Cardassian's teeth ground together. No diversion, then. No intervention at all.

As much as it galled him, he had no choice but to accept the situation—and hope he would eventually find a way to turn it to his advantage.

Guinan was still reeling from her experience in the footwear emporium, or she would have noticed it moments earlier.

Crowds had a certain sound to them—raucous, subdued, or any of a hundred flavors in between. And not every part of a crowd sounded like every other.

When she and Picard walked into the shop, the crowd of merchants on both sides of the thoroughfare had sounded exactly as she would have expected—a mix of purposefulness and pleasure, with accents of happiness or remorse over deals that had either been cut or abandoned.

But it sounded different now. There were dead spots in the crowd, places where people were simply watching and not speaking. And no sooner had Guinan realized this than the dead spots began to migrate.

Not randomly, either. They were converging on a single point. And the point they were converging on was Guinan herself.

Security officers, she told herself, feeling ice water trickle down her spine. She and her companion had been discovered somehow, despite their disguises.

"Picard," she breathed.

He looked at her. "Yes?"

"Don't look now, but we're surrounded."

His brow lowered. "By whom?"

"Security," she said. Then she added, "I think," because she couldn't be completely sure, and because her talents weren't as sharp as they used to be.

"Just keep walking," Picard told her.

Guinan could almost hear him add: *I'll think of something*.

And despite the severity of their circumstances, despite the odds stacked against them, Guinan had a feeling that Picard *would* think of something.

After all, he was the man who had saved her life more than four hundred years ago. If he could get the better of those time-traveling snakes in San Francisco, he could get them out of this mess as well.

Guinan looked to him, wondering what her companion was going to do next—wondering what kind of rabbit he was going to pull out of his hat.

But Picard didn't produce any rabbits. All he did, suddenly and without warning, was take off like one—cutting a path among the assembled merchants without so much as a backward look.

Guinan didn't understand. It looked to her as if her friend was abandoning her.

No, she thought. *That can't be it.* It was just a ruse, designed to fool the security officers.

But she was too smart to believe in it. She knew Picard. She knew he wouldn't let her down.

Then a couple of figures closed in on her, phasers in their fists. Even if they weren't in uniform, it was obvious that they were security officers.

"Don't move!" one of them barked.

Okay, Guinan thought, *it's time, Picard. Show these guys what you've got.*

But her companion wasn't stopping. As she watched, he became more and more a part of the crowd. By the time the ripples of what was happening to her began to spread through the shopping area, Picard was gone altogether.

Guinan swallowed back her shock and disappointment. It hadn't been a ruse after all. Picard had really run away, leaving her there to face the music by herself.

A couple of other armed figures joined the first two, blocking Guinan's escape on all sides. "Hands up!" one of them snapped at her. "Stay where you are!"

It wasn't necessary. She wasn't going anywhere.

Chapter Fourteen

PICARD LOOKED BACK OVER his shoulder to see if anyone was pushing through the crowd to come after him.

No one was—at least, as far as he could tell. The authorities seemed to be focusing all their attention on Guinan, the proverbial bird in the hand.

The captain frowned as he headed for the hatch that would let him out of the shopping enclosure. Obviously, Steej had caught on to them. Having heard reports of a couple of nosy Cataxxans, he must have eventually put two and two together.

And now he had snared one of them.

If Picard was to keep Steej from snaring the other, he had to adopt a different approach. It was no longer enough for him to pose as a Cataxxan. Now he had to conceal that identity every bit as zealously as his own, or find himself sharing a detention cell with Guinan.

As for locating Demmix...the difficulty factor had been raised considerably. After all, the captain would be looking over his shoulder the whole time. There were only so many Cataxxans in the city, and Steej's officers would be seeking one who fit the captain's general description.

Picard's only logical course of action was to abandon his mission and ask Ben Zoma to beam him out. But he wasn't going to give Demmix up so easily.

And he wasn't going to give Guinan up at all.

It didn't matter what it cost him to free her. She had risked her life to break him out of his cell. He would be damned if he wasn't going to return the favor.

As Picard thought that, he emerged from the hatch into the next hull—one of the seedier-looking ones he had seen in Oblivion. It housed a multitude of tiny shops, quite a few of them empty—the result of business failures, apparently, since they showed evidence of having been occupied once.

More important, there was no sign of Steej's men—at least, not in uniform. But the captain couldn't rule out the possibility of undercover officers like the ones who had come after him and his companion.

Pulling his collar up around his ears and looking down as much as possible, he made his way through the maze. Fortunately for him, it was a lot less populated than the adjoining hull, so there were fewer people around to identify him.

This place also appeared less reputable than the shopping area. Picard got the feeling that the people he passed here didn't care whether he was a fugitive or not, and might even have been fugitives themselves once.

He hoped that was the case. Obviously, that sort of atmosphere would work in his favor.

Still, Picard hadn't gotten more than halfway through the maze when he sensed that someone was following him. His first impulse was to run again, but he contained it.

After all, no one had accused him of anything, or ordered him to stop. For all he knew, it wasn't even the authorities behind him. It might have been someone else entirely, with an agenda he hadn't even considered.

In any case, the captain didn't think it would hurt to take a look.

Glancing back over his shoulder, he saw a quartet of Cardassians. Normally, they wouldn't have represented any particular danger to him.

But he had learned that there were Cardassians on Demmix's trail, searching for the Zartani just as Picard was. And if he had heard about *them*, they could as easily have heard about *him*.

His expression must have betrayed his thoughts, because one of the Cardassians chose that moment to reach into his tunic and pull out a hand weapon.

Picard was still armed, but he didn't want to get into a phaser battle—not with the numbers game quite clearly in his adversaries' favor. And even if he emerged the winner, it would only attract attention to him.

So he took the only other course open to him. He made a run for it, as he had in the shopping area.

There was a moment when the captain was certain he

was going to be hit with a disruptor beam squarely in the back. Then the moment passed and he was tearing around a corner, following the idiosyncrasies of the maze.

With a chorus of muffled curses, the Cardassians came after him. But Picard had been a fair runner at one time, and the maze assisted him by keeping his pursuers from getting a clear shot at him.

He was thinking he could get out of this bind, embracing the possibility that he could reach the next hatch and lose the Cardassians somewhere down the line. Then he turned a corner and ran into something that changed his mind for him—something not only unexpected, but hard and unyielding.

It took the captain a moment to realize that it was another Cardassian. That's when it occurred to him that he had been caught in a vise.

And for all he knew, there might be more Cardassians on their way. With that thought spurring him on, he drove his fist into his enemy's face, sending him staggering.

But by then, the Cardassian quartet had caught up with him, as evidenced by a hard-driven shoulder in the small of his back. It propelled him forward, slamming him face-first into the wall of an empty shop.

Picard tasted blood, but didn't let it slow him down. Swinging his elbow back as hard as he could, he struck his attacker in the mouth. And as the Cardassian let go of him, he reached into his tunic for his phaser.

But as he pulled it out, another adversary sent him spinning with a blow to the jaw. By the time the captain regained his equilibrium, his weapon was gone. And there wasn't any time to look for it, because the Cardassian who had hit him was coming at him again.

But Picard had no intention of becoming the fellow's punching bag. Rocking back on one foot, he lashed out with his other one and caught his attacker in the throat.

Uttering a strangled cry, the Cardassian collapsed, giving Picard some hope of escape. But it was dashed when another Cardassian crashed into him and bore him to the deck.

Twisting in his assailant's grasp, Picard struck him in the face. Unfortunately, it didn't make the Cardassian let go. If anything, it made him hold on to the captain more tenaciously. And a moment later, another Cardassian grabbed the wrist that had launched the blow.

Picard did his best to defend himself with the single hand left to him, but it didn't work very well. Before too long, someone shot a bolt of pain into his ribs with a well-placed kick, and then another and another.

Then he was dragged across the floor. Into one of the empty storefronts, no doubt.

By then he was on the verge of losing consciousness. But just as he began to sink into a swirling darkness, he felt himself lifted by the front of his tunic.

"Look at me," someone growled, and shook him.

Opening his eyes, Picard saw a face swimming in front of him. There was no question in his mind that this was the Cardassians' leader. The captain could see it in the angle of his jaw, in his bearing, in every aspect of his appearance.

He was clearly an individual to be reckoned with.

And at the moment, with a trio of armed subordinates standing behind him, he held all the cards.

"Your name is Picard," he said.

The captain neither confirmed it nor denied it. But inwardly, he acknowledged the efficacy of his adversary's intelligence systems.

"Where is Demmix?" the Cardassian asked, in a surprisingly reasonable tone of voice.

Picard's jaw clenched. "I wish I knew."

The Cardassian considered him for a moment, as if Picard were some new species of fauna. Then he struck the human with his fist, snapping Picard's head back.

"I'll ask again," he said. "Where is Demmix?"

The captain spat out the blood he felt welling in his mouth. "I don't know. And your striking me is not going to make me any more knowledgeable."

The Cardassian eyed him. "Maybe not. Maybe this is an exercise in futility."

Then he bludgeoned Picard again, driving bone into bone with agonizing results.

"On the other hand," the Cardassian added, "I have nothing to lose by continuing it...do I?"

Once more, he pulled his fist back. But before he could make use of it to punish Picard, the captain thought of a more desirable alternative.

"Wait!" he cried out.

The Cardassian held back, his eyes narrowing. "You have something to say after all?"

The captain drew a deep, shuddering breath. "Hear me out—please. I honestly do not know where Demmix is hiding."

His interrogator sighed and struck him again, opening a fiery cut beneath his eye.

"But," Picard continued, knowing full well the significance of what he was about to say, "my *companion* knows."

"Your companion?" Tain echoed. "You mean the one the authorities caught a moment ago?"

The captain nodded. "Yes. Her name is...Guinan."

For maybe the fiftieth time that night, Nikolas turned over in his bed and offered himself up to sleep. Unfortunately, sleep refused to cooperate.

It wasn't bad enough that he kept torturing himself with thoughts of Gerda Idun. Now he had a nemesis in the form of Lieutenant Hanta to worry about.

The Bolian was strong, too. Stronger than most any human. If Nikolas was going to avoid getting his butt kicked, he was going to have to put Hanta back on his heels. That meant being quicker, more aggressive—establishing who was boss right from the get-go.

And the ensign would do those things. In fact, it would be his pleasure.

Just then, the doors to his quarters slid apart, and something moved through the darkness. It didn't stop until it reached the room's other bed.

It was Paris, of course. But Nikolas wasn't used to seeing him get in so late. He wondered what could have kept a straight arrow like Paris from going to bed at his regular time.

A late-night warp-propulsion seminar? A monograph on thruster response times?

Paris wasn't exactly a live wire, which was why their relationship had only been a cordial one. Not that Nikolas had anything against the guy. It was just that he liked things with a little more edge to them.

Or had. Now nothing got him going—nothing except the memory of Gerda Idun disappearing in front of his eyes.

Though unaware of Nikolas's pain, Paris pulled his covers aside slowly and carefully. Obviously, he was trying to get into bed without making any noise.

But he had probably grown up in a family where people were considerate about letting each other sleep. When Nikolas was growing up, there had been no chance of that. If a person got some peace and quiet in the morning, it could only mean the rest of the family was gone for the weekend.

Suddenly, Nikolas heard a thump, followed by a half-stifled cry of pain. Under different circumstances, he would have found some humor in the fact.

But not now. Nothing seemed funny to him these days.

"It's all right," he said, letting his roommate off the hook. "I'm awake."

Paris let out a sigh of relief. "Well, that's good. Maybe I can get into bed with one shin still intact."

Sarcasm, thought Nikolas. Paris hadn't been capable of it when he first moved in. Obviously, Nikolas had an influence on him after all, even if it often seemed that the guy was barely listening to him.

He waited for Paris to get into bed and get comfortable. Then he turned to the wall, dragged his covers around him, and tried again to get some sleep.

But for what seemed like a long time, it continued to elude him. And Nikolas cringed at the prospect of reciting the periodic table again.

Just as he was about to give up the struggle and get dressed to stalk the corridors, he heard something—a whisper. And it seemed to be coming from Paris.

No, Nikolas thought. *It can't be.* Paris never said anything after he got into bed. *Never.* Hell, as far as Nikolas could tell, the guy never made small talk at all.

Then Nikolas heard it again.

Looking back over his shoulder, he saw Paris's silhouette in the darkness. The guy was propped up on one elbow, looking a lot like somebody who wanted to talk.

Nikolas turned around the rest of the way and said, "Did you just ask me something?"

There was silence for a moment—almost long enough for Nikolas to believe he was mistaken after all. Then Paris said, "I was just asking what you thought of Jiterica."

Nikolas hadn't given her much thought. He said so.

"I mean," said Paris, "have you ever thought about her as something more than…" He seemed to struggle for a moment. "More than a *friend,*" he said finally.

Nikolas wondered if the guy was joking. If so, it would be a first for him.

"More than a friend," Nikolas echoed.

"Yes. More like…" Another generous dollop of silence. "Like a romantic attachment."

Nikolas had to wonder if they were talking about the same Jiterica. The one he knew was a low-density being, who couldn't even remain in anything approaching humanoid form without the help of a special containment suit.

"Do you know what you're talking about?" he had to ask.

"I know," said Paris. "It sounds insane. But I think I've got feelings for her."

Nikolas didn't know what to say.

"And," his roommate continued, "I think she's got feelings for me too."

Oh, man, thought Nikolas. *Do you have any idea what you're letting yourself in for?*

"Part of me knows we're headed for trouble," said Paris. "But another part of me doesn't care. I just want to be with her, no matter how difficult it may be."

It sounded familiar.

"Do you know what I mean?" Paris asked, the tremor of real pain in his voice.

All too well, Nikolas thought.

"If you were me," Paris asked, "what would *you* do?"

Nikolas's first impulse was to tell his roommate to bark up another tree. Interspecies romances were common enough, but not when one of the partners was human and the other was basically a coherent ion cloud.

Then he remembered how much he wanted Gerda Idun—even when he knew she would eventually go back to her own universe, even when he knew what kind of mission she was on.

Nikolas had been willing to accept any hardship, any sacrifice, if it meant being with her. So who was he to tell Paris to play it safe?

"If I were you," Nikolas said, "I'd follow my instincts—wherever they led me."

Paris seemed to consider the advice for a moment. Then he said, "Thanks." Just that.

But what it *really* sounded like was "I think you're right. I'll give it a shot."

"No problem," said Nikolas.

It was funny. Paris was about to embark on what had to be one of the unlikeliest love affairs in the history of Man. He was about to take on all kinds of frustrations, all kinds of disappointments.

And Nikolas envied him like crazy.

Enabran Tain scowled as he considered Picard in the confines of the abandoned shop.

From what he had seen of humans, they were soft, squeamish, and entirely too interested in their own preservation. In fact, it was a puzzle to him how they could even walk erect.

Picard, who was clearly human despite the purple dye in his skin, couldn't have been blessed with much more fortitude than the rest of his species, and he had to know what kind of punishment his captors could dispense if they chose to do so.

So the last thing he should have wanted to do was anger them. And yet, he persisted in his claim that he didn't know the whereabouts of the Zartani—and that only his companion, Guinan, could help Tain with that information.

The only reasonable conclusion was that Picard was telling the truth. But if that was the case, it presented the Cardassian with a rather sizable problem.

After all, Guinan was by now in the clutches of Commander Steej and his security people. That meant that she would soon be placed in Steej's detention facility, if she hadn't been already.

A couple of days earlier, it might not have been so difficult to break her out of the place. Indeed, she had broken Picard out of it all by herself.

But now that Guinan's actions had highlighted the facility's weaknesses, security measures there would be a lot more stringent. There would be more guards on hand, more supervision, and more attention paid to surveillance systems.

It seemed an impossibility that Tain and his men could free Picard's companion. Were it not for the magnitude of the stakes, the glinn wouldn't even have considered it.

But the human seemed to have a plan in mind.

"Elaborate," said Tain.

Picard glanced at Beylen and Karrid, who were standing behind him, as if trying to make sure they weren't going to kill him before he answered.

"Speak," Tain told him.

"The detention facility," said Picard, "is actually an old Chezzulid battle cruiser—I noticed that when I was inside. It was one of the vessels I was compelled to commit to memory when I studied ship design at Starfleet Academy."

Interesting, Tain thought. "Go on."

"Since then," said the human, "I've had occasion to board one of them. It was a derelict, just like the one we are discussing. The crew was dead, victims of a radiation leak, so we had ample time to look around."

"And what did you find?" asked Tain, less than interested in Picard's adventures.

"They're difficult to break out of," said Picard, "but not nearly as difficult to break *into*."

"Why is that?" asked the glinn.

"There's a raised spine that runs around the outside of the hull, designed to house certain power-distribution conduits. Of course, the Chezzulid needed access to those conduits in case something malfunctioned."

"And do you know how they arranged that access?" asked Tain.

"I do," said Picard.

"So you can get us into that spine?"

The human nodded. "Yes."

"How close can we get to your friend?" Tain asked.

"Close enough to touch her," said Picard, "if not for the bulkhead separating her from us."

"Which we can break through with our disruptors," the glinn said, picturing it.

"That is the idea," the human agreed.

"But we will have to move quickly," said Tain. "Otherwise, Steej's men will be on top of us."

"More than likely," said Picard, "the majority of Steej's officers will be deployed at the entrance to the detention facility. They will not expect a problem to emerge from the direction of my friend's cell."

It makes sense, the glinn thought.

"And even after they have determined what is happening," said Picard, "it will not be easy for them. The entrance to the room that contains Guinan's cell is a narrow one. Steej's men will not be able to get inside it all at once—especially if they have to worry about being fired upon."

"And by then, we may be gone."

"Precisely," said Picard.

The more Tain heard, the more he liked the idea.

"There's just one problem," said the human. "The Chezzulid are not exactly masters of warp-drive mechanics. The only way they can muster enough power for faster-than-light travel is to cheat in the area of life supports."

"What does that mean?" asked Tain.

"It means they only have heat where it is absolutely necessary. The rest of the vessel is allowed to drop to a temperature well below freezing."

The glinn scowled. He found Oblivion cold *enough*, and it was generally kept at a temperature most species considered comfortable. He cringed at the prospect of moving through an environment with hardly any heat at all.

On the other hand, he had a mission to carry out. He wasn't eager to tell his superiors that he had let his personal comfort come before his duty.

"That's not an obstacle," he said.

Picard nodded. "Good. The other thing you will want to know is that the spaces we will be passing through are rather narrow." He took in the Cardassians at a glance. "I doubt that all of you will make it through."

The glinn considered his men, of whom there were

now six. A couple of them *were* rather fleshy, now that he thought about it.

Fortunately, Tain himself was in good shape. He wouldn't be one of those forced to stay behind.

"Then we won't all go," he said.

"As long as you accept that," said Picard.

"How soon can we do this?" asked the Cardassian.

After all, time was a factor. If the authorities had closed in on Picard and his friend for asking questions, Tain and his underlings might become their next targets.

Picard shrugged. "Now, if you like."

Tain nodded. "Let's get started."

The human held his hand out. "I will need my weapon back."

"For what purpose?" Tain wondered.

"We are breaking into a heavily guarded detention facility."

"And?" asked the glinn.

"And what if Steej's men fire at me?"

"Then," said Tain, "I expect you'll die. Or at the least, sustain painful injuries."

The human made a face. "I am not terribly fond of either outcome."

"How fond are you of dying here and now in this abandoned shop?" the glinn asked.

Picard glanced at Karrid and Beylen again. "Point taken," he said.

"Then we're agreed," said Tain.

"Yes." The human started for the exit.

"Just one other thing," said the glinn.

Picard looked back at him.

"If at any time I even suspect you're trying to deceive me, I will put a burning hole in your back the size of your head. Is that clear?"

"Quite clear," the human assured him.

"Then let's go," said Tain.

Chapter Fifteen

GUINAN SAT IN THE SAME CELL Picard had occupied the day before, looking out through a transparent barrier at a portion of Commander Steej's dentention facility.

It looked different from this perspective. And not in a good way, she remarked inwardly.

She had known, when she set out to free Picard, that she might wind up in a place like this. But she hadn't appreciated the hard, unyielding reality of it.

For all Guinan's experience and abilities, this wasn't something she was going to be able to get out of. This was, quite possibly, the end of the line for her.

She would be judged and, more than likely, found guilty of her crimes. And since Oblivion didn't have the resources to keep people incarcerated on a long-term basis, she would be sent to a mining colony, where she would spend the rest of her days dragging useful minerals out of the ground.

Then Guinan would die, because even El-Aurians died eventually. And that would be it.

But the worst part, the absolute nadir of the entire ordeal, was that she couldn't work up the emotion to care. After all, the one thing she had allowed herself to care about had turned out to be unworthy of the effort.

Feeling more desolate than ever, Guinan drew her knees up to her chest and wrapped her arms around them. At the same time, she noticed that the guards outside her cell had been joined by another security officer.

No, she realized. Not just another officer.

It was Steej. She recognized him from their encounter outside the detention facility. And having turned toward her, he was peering at her through the energy wall of her cell.

He seemed to be picking her apart with his eyes. She didn't like it. However, under the circumstances, there wasn't a great deal she could do about it.

Steej waited until one of his officers deactivated the transparent barrier for him. Then he entered Guinan's cell, sat down on its other chair, and met her gaze.

"I am Commander Steej," he said, in a serene, almost musical voice. "But then, you probably know that."

Guinan nodded.

"And as you must also know," he said, with the slightest undercurrent of anger, "you are in a great deal of trouble—not only with the law here in Oblivion, which is bad enough, but also with *me*."

She nodded again.

Steej tilted his head. "What's your name?"

She couldn't see what difference it would make if she gave it to him. "Guinan."

His brow wrinkled. "Guinan... ?"

"Just Guinan."

"I see." He regarded her with his dark, protuberant eyes. "An interesting disguise, Guinan. One must look closely to see that you are not a Cataxxan."

Reluctant to go down that road lest she get her friend Dahlen in trouble, Guinan didn't say anything in response. She just sat there, waiting for whatever came next.

"You took a rather large risk," the Rythrian observed, "first, in helping Mister Hill escape from us, and then in helping him to elude us."

Guinan remained silent.

Her interrogator leaned closer to her. "What, exactly, is your relationship to Mister Hill?"

She thought she had known the answer to that question. But obviously she had been mistaken.

Steej was waiting for a response. "We're just... acquaintances," Guinan told him.

"Acquaintances?" the security director echoed. "And yet, you went to the trouble of helping him break out of this detention facility. If you go to such lengths for your acquaintances, what do you do for your friends?"

Not much, she thought. *At least, not lately.* But she had begun to diverge from that behavior when it came to Picard.

"I'll ask you again," Steej told her. "What is your relationship to Mister Hill?"

What could Guinan say? That she had encountered

him hundreds of years earlier, and felt grateful for
kindness he showed her? That his very presence
given her hope?

And that everything she felt about him had b
ground to ashes when she saw him run away?

"We met in a bar," she said, "shortly before the bo
went off. Based on what I knew of him, I didn't think
was the one who set it off."

The Rythrian nodded as if he understood. "His ar
offended your sense of fair play, your sense of just
So you risked your life to set him free—this person
met in a bar just a few minutes earlier."

Suddenly, Guinan felt the sting of her interrogat
hand striking her face.

Steej leaned even closer. "If I were you, I would
consider my situation, and the advisability of lyin
someone who holds my fate in his hands."

Just then, one of his officers came to the barrier
gestured. Frowning, the security director gestured b;
and the officer deactivated the barrier.

"Luck is with you," Steej told Guinan. "You've b
given a respite. But I'll be back."

And with that, he left the cell.

Guinan touched her cheek where the Rythrian hac
her. It was hot and sore to the touch.

But it could have been worse. And it would be, if
didn't come up with an answer Steej liked.

She sat back and closed her eyes, and thought,
card, what have you done to me?

Guinan understood why he had left her—or thou
she did. It was for the sake of his mission.

But the Picard she knew back in San Francisco had placed her above his mission—above even his life. At least, that was the way she remembered it.

I guess I was wrong about him, she conceded with a pang of regret. *I gave him too much credit. I believed in him.*

And now she was paying the price for her credulity.

Ben Zoma looked across the captain's sleek, black desk at Lieutenant Kastiigan. "So," he said, like a man about to activate a phaser while peering blithely into its emitter, "what did you want to talk about?"

He knew the Kandilkari well enough to have some idea of where their conversation was headed. However, Kastiigan was the chief science officer on the *Stargazer,* and Ben Zoma couldn't deny him a chance to speak—as much as he might have wanted to.

Kastiigan looked vaguely conspiratorial as he leaned over the edge of the desk. "It's no secret that Captain Picard's mission in Oblivion has gone awry somehow. The only thing we don't know yet is how *far* awry."

Ben Zoma nodded. "Fair enough."

The sciences chief seemed encouraged by the comment. Of course, Ben Zoma mused, he would probably have found a way to continue even if Ben Zoma had told him he was crazy.

"As the captain himself informed us," said Kastiigan, "he is the only individual capable of carrying out this mission. That is why he entered Oblivion alone. However, if we have not heard from him—neither at the ap-

pointed time nor since—should we not be consider
the notion of sending in a rescue team?"

Ben Zoma looked at his colleague askance. It hac
taken him long, had it?

Ever since his arrival on the ship, Kastiigan had b
lobbying for a chance to risk his life. The reason fc
almost didn't seem to matter why. All that mattered v
that his hide would be in jeopardy.

"I take it," said Ben Zoma, "that you want to be p
of this rescue team?"

The science officer blinked. "Actually, no."

The first officer wasn't sure he had heard correc
"You don't?"

"Not at all," Kastiigan said. "There aren't any n
chant traders among my people. A Kandilkari in Ob
ion would stick out like…what is the expression y
humans have? Like a damaged appendage?"

"A sore thumb?" Ben Zoma suggested.

"Yes," said Kastiigan. "Like a sore thumb, exactly.
you can see why it might not be advisable for me to p
ticipate in the captain's rescue."

Ben Zoma nodded. "Absolutely."

The Kandilkari's brow furrowed. "I hope you wer
counting on me in that regard—as part of a res
team."

"No," the first officer assured him. "Not at all."

He didn't get it. Kastiigan was declining an invitat
to risk his neck even before Ben Zoma had extende
to him. It made him wonder why Kastiigan had bothe
to raise the topic in the first place.

He asked the science officer that very question.

"Because I'm concerned about the captain," Kasti-igan said congenially, "just as everyone else is."

Ben Zoma supposed it was possible. "I see."

Kastiigan looked pleased. "Good. So what do you think?"

The human had to pause for a second to remember what he meant. "You mean...about a rescue mission?"

"That's correct."

"I'm considering it," Ben Zoma said. "But at the moment, I'm still hoping it won't become necessary."

"As we all are," Kastiigan noted.

"But thanks for your input," Ben Zoma told him.

The science officer shrugged. "I see it as my responsibility to advise my superiors however and wherever I can."

Ben Zoma smiled. "That's very dutiful of you."

"It is then up to you," Kastiigan continued, "to accept or reject that advice."

"I'm glad you see it that way," said the first officer, coming around the captain's desk to escort his colleague to the door. "Now, if you don't mind, I have some—"

"Of course," said Kastiigan, "there is the matter of the *Lake-Dweller-That-Roars.*"

Ben Zoma stopped halfway around the desk. "The *Lake-Dweller-That-Roars...?*"

"Yes. She's a Kandilkari vessel, named after a rare but wonderful denizen of a lake near my childhood home. Like so many other onetime titans of the spaceways, she became absorbed into Oblivion many years ago."

Ben Zoma knew he would regret asking, but he couldn't let it go by. "What's this got to do with the captain?"

"Well," said Kastiigan, "my people's early spacefaring vessels are something of a hobby with me. It wouldn't be difficult for me to activate some of her dormant tactical systems from afar and provide a rather sensational distraction, while a rescue team goes in and finds the captain."

It wasn't a terrible idea. "I'll keep that in mind," said Ben Zoma. "In case we need a distraction, that is."

And, strangely enough, it didn't involve Kastiigan putting his life on the line. After all, he would be activating the vessel's systems from a remote location.

It hardly seemed possible, but Kastiigan had made two entire suggestions without either of them putting him at risk. Ben Zoma was beginning to get the feeling that he had misjudged the sciences chief.

Kastiigan got up to go. "I will be in my section if you have need of me."

"I'll remember that," the first officer said.

The Kandilkari was halfway to the door before he turned and said, "By the way, Ensign Jiterica has detected the presence of an Ubarrak warship."

That got Ben Zoma's attention. "Where?"

"Approximately twenty billion kilometers from here. You see," said Kastiigan, warming to his subject, "the ensign was studying the behavioral nuances of the star in this system, and she noticed something just inside the edge of its corona.

"Now, if I were to take a shuttle a bit closer to the Ubarrak vessel, using the corona as cover, I could attempt to determine their intentions. And if they were to respond to my maneuver in a hostile manner, I could simply—"

The first officer held his hand up. "Hang on. Twenty billion kilometers isn't cause for concern, Kastiigan—especially when you consider the fact that most Ubarrak transports travel with a military escort. She's probably just waiting for her date to leave Oblivion."

The science officer was clearly disappointed. "I see. In that case, I'll make our scrutiny of the vessel less of a priority."

"That would be best," said Ben Zoma.

"However," said Kastiigan, "if you think of some other effort in which lives must be placed at risk—"

"I'll put your name at the top of the list. I promise."

"Thank you," said the science officer. Finally, he walked out of the room.

As soon as he was gone, Ben Zoma chuckled to himself. He was relieved that Kastiigan had finally volunteered for his customary suicide mission.

Otherwise, he would have felt compelled to see if the stars were falling from the heavens.

Picard hadn't been lying about the idiosyncrasies of Chezzulid ship design. The tube through which he and his Cardassian allies were crawling was narrow, awkwardly shaped, and colder than anything he might ever have imagined.

It hurt even to breathe, each intake of air cutting like a knife. The skin of his face felt stretched to its limits. And he had to be careful not to let his hands linger on any exposed metal, lest he lose a layer of skin.

All the more reason to move quickly, the captain told himself, his breath freezing in the air in front of him.

All the more reason to remember where he was going—and why.

But it wasn't just the cold that was exacting its pound of flesh. His knees and shins, protected only by the fabric of his pants, were taking a beating from a multitude of protruding ridges and cable clamps.

Picard's only consolation was that the Cardassians were feeling the same discomfort. In fact, their colder-blooded constitutions were probably getting along even worse under these conditions than his was.

He looked back over his shoulder and saw all three of them—the one called Tain, who was obviously in charge, and two of his more slender lackeys. They were all armed, ready to kill their temporary ally at a moment's notice.

And there was little to stop them. He had already shown them how to reach Guinan. Tain's flat, handheld sensor device would let him know when they got to precisely the right spot. And now that they were almost there, they didn't need Picard to break into his friend's cell.

But he had been in Steej's detention facility and they hadn't, so he knew the place better than they did. And as well, they had to be concerned that Guinan wouldn't go with them unless she saw a familiar face.

That was all that was keeping him alive, the captain suspected. Once the Cardassians got Guinan out of the tube, he was probably as good as dead.

"Halt!" snapped a voice behind him.

He turned and saw Tain training his sensor on the conduit-covered bulkhead to their right. Slowly, the Cardassian tracked forward with the device, stopping only after it was pointed at a spot roughly even with Picard's shoulder.

The Cardassian looked up from his readout and gestured with two of his fingers. "There," he said. "That's her."

He could say for certain because he had taken a reading of Guinan—as well as Picard—shortly before Steej's men moved in on them. Or so the Cardassian had said.

In any case, they had come about the right distance. More than likely, Tain was right, and Guinan's cell was a mere bulkhead's width away.

Luckily, there was a space between the conduits big enough to facilitate an escape. Without any encouragement from Picard, Tain put his sensor away and took out his disruptor. Then he trained it on the curve of the bulkhead and fired an intense, narrow beam, raising a stream of white vapor where it struck.

But this wasn't really a bulkhead. In truth, it was the vessel's hull, the spine in which they were hiding being a mere add-on without any structural significance. Even at his weapon's highest setting, it would take the Cardassian as much as thirty seconds to punch his way through.

Picard wished he could communicate with Guinan somehow, let her know what was going on. But it wasn't an option. He just had to hope she would understand the significance of the hole when it appeared, and keep her guards from discovering it until it was too late.

Meanwhile, Tain dug into layer after layer of metal alloy, his face thrown into sharp relief by the pale blue light of his beam. And all the while, the cold took up residence in their bones like an unwanted visitor.

Finally, the bulkhead seemed to boil under the influence of the disruptor, as its last few molecules lost their integrity. Then the final layer of metal vanished, leaving a hole the size of Picard's thumbnail.

Tain deactivated his beam and gestured for the captain to attempt verbal contact. Picard put his face near the hole, which still stank of burning metal, and made a hissing sound.

Then he said, "Guinan? Can you hear me?"

There was no response—at least, not at first. Then the captain heard his friend say, "Picard?"

She sounded surprised to see him. But then, the captain mused, *Who wouldn't be surprised?*

"Indeed. Have any of your guards noticed anything yet?"

"Not yet," said Guinan.

"With luck," he said, "it will remain that way. Just stay away from the bulkhead, all right? I wouldn't want you to be struck by the beam."

"I understand," she said.

His message sent, Picard pulled his head back and gave Tain access to the bulkhead again. This time, the Cardassian expanded the scope of his beam as much as possible and leaned back against the opposite surface before he pressed the trigger.

With more area to cover, the disruptor beam would take longer to achieve its objective. However, it was the only realistic option they had.

The alternative would have been to stay with a narrow-aperture beam and try to carve a chunk out of the metal surface. But that would have been visible from

Guinan's cell for too long a period of time—and when they were finished, they would still have had a sizable section of bulkhead to push out.

Entire minutes passed while Tain's beam ate at the barrier, turning it into vapor. But after a while, his shivering began to make his beam quiver as well.

"I could take over," Picard suggested, though he was shivering by then as much as Tain was.

The Cardassian shot him a dirty look. Then he turned back to his work on the bulkhead.

Finally, the last of the metal surface sizzled away, giving them a window on Guinan's cell. And from where Picard sat, he couldn't see any guards.

"Get her," Tain growled, his teeth clenched against the cold.

Picard extended himself through the opening, grateful that the edges made by the disruptor were smooth and not jagged, and more warm than hot. As his upper body emerged into the cell, he saw Guinan standing by the wall.

And no guards, even on the other side of the energy barrier. Their luck was holding.

But Picard didn't think that state of affairs would go on for long. Steej's people were bound to look in on the prisoner eventually. And when they did, they would see she was being spirited away behind their backs.

"Come on," he said to Guinan, and held out his hand.

Taking it, she let the captain help her through the aperture. It was only after they were both inside the tube that she realized they weren't alone.

Guinan turned to him, her expression that of someone who felt betrayed.

"It's all right," Picard told her. "They are on our side." *At least for now,* he added silently, unable to elaborate in the presence of the Cardassians.

"Come on," Tain rasped.

He didn't look happy. But then, his upper lip had begun to frost over and he was trembling uncontrollably.

As the Cardassian and his men began to crawl away, Guinan fell in line with them. But before she could get very far, Picard grabbed her arm and thrust himself ahead of her.

He knew that he had to act quickly, before Tain—who was on all fours up ahead of him—could see what was happening. Otherwise, the captain would be sealing his death and, eventually, his friend's as well.

Shooting forward, Picard shoved Tain into a protruding conduit as hard as he could. Then, before the Cardassian could recover, the captain leaped on him and snatched his disruptor out of his hand.

Tain cried out, alerting his underlings to what had happened. But by then, Picard was pulling back, weapon in hand.

As the Cardassians struggled to get a shot at him in the confines of the tube, the captain aimed his disruptor at a stretch of conduits that sat between him and Tain. Then he fired.

Instantly, the passageway filled with sparks and a white-hot cloud of gas, cutting the Cardassians off from Picard's view. He took the opportunity to urge Guinan in the other direction.

"That way!" he told her. "And hurry!"

She moved as quickly as she could, with the captain

right behind her. As he passed the hole in the wall of Guinan's cell, he allowed himself a look inside.

There was still no sign that anyone had noticed her absence. That was good, Picard told himself, as he left the escape hole behind. They needed all the head start they could get.

Meanwhile, he could hear the Cardassians' cries of outrage behind them. But they wouldn't be able to follow—not with all that flesh-searing plasma in the way.

Eventually, they would see that they had no choice but to retrace their steps, even if they had lost the prize they came for. After all, it was preferable to getting caught.

But Tain had to be wondering what Picard had accomplished. By cutting himself off from the Cardassians, it must have seemed he had also cut himself off from his escape route.

Of course, that wasn't quite true.

What Picard hadn't told Tain was that the spine of the Chezzulid ship had more than one opening. In fact, the one for which he was headed was actually a bit closer than the one he had entered by.

Suddenly, he heard Guinan hiss at him over the greater hiss of escaping plasma. Looking back, the captain saw her pump her thumb over her shoulder, a look of anxiety on her face.

Her message was clear. Steej's security people had discovered that she was missing, or were about to.

Picard hadn't heard any sounds to support that observation—not yet, at least. However, Guinan had already proven that her powers of perception were superior to his own. If she believed her captors were on to them, he certainly wasn't going to debate the matter with her.

Stopping and turning, he took aim at another conduit—this time, one that was almost directly in line with Guinan's escape hole. Then he sent a spear of disruptor energy into it, creating a second sibilant plasma cloud as big as the first.

Of course, Steej's security officers might still be tempted to fire blindly through the roil of gases—and since Guinan had no weapon, Picard was the only one who could fire back at them. With that in mind, he stood his ground for the moment and let his companion crawl on.

You know, he complained to himself, *it is even colder in this place when one stops moving.*

That was when he heard the shouts and curses of Steej's officers—just as Guinan had warned. But he didn't see any resulting energy beams.

Maybe Steej's men were afraid that they would ignite the plasma, or else accidentally poke a hole in the vessel's hull. No matter the reason, Picard was glad of it.

Making haste again, he caught up with Guinan. "Not too much farther now," he told her.

"Good," she said. "If I had known it was going to be this cold, I might have stayed in my cell."

A joke, Picard thought.

It was strange that Guinan should choose this place and time to make one, when she had been so somber since the moment he met her. Perhaps it was just a release of anxiety.

Yes, he told himself. *That's it. What other explanation can there be?*

After a moment, Guinan spoke up again. "I think I see something up ahead."

"Something that looks like a handle?" the captain asked.

"Yes, I think so."

The exit, he thought.

"That is where we get off," he told Guinan.

"Not a moment too soon," she returned.

A few moments later, they reached it—a round hatch in the floor of the tube with an L-shaped metal handle. A few turns and they would be out.

Picard put his disruptor down and tried to do the honors. But he couldn't get a grip on the thing. His hands were too frozen, too clawlike.

He looked up at Guinan, his tongue thick and unresponsive. "C-can you...?"

"Clockwise or counter?" she asked, trails of white steam streaming from her mouth.

"Cl-clockwise," the captain told her.

Without another word, Guinan put her hands on the handle and bent to the task. And though she must have been devilishly cold as well, she managed to turn the handle—once, twice, and then a third time.

"Now pull it toward you," he told her.

With the creak of an undoubtedly long-neglected hinge, the hatch came open. Picard could feel the welcome rush of warm air in his face.

"A-after you," he said.

He watched her lower herself through the opening to

the deck below—apparently without anyone's notice. Scooping up his disruptor in his hands, he tossed it down to her. Then he lowered himself through the hatch as well.

The captain found himself in an irregularly shaped, unused, and unoccupied section of the Chezzulid vessel—one that Steej must have known about but ignored.

And for the first time since Guinan had crawled out of her detention cell, he was able to look at her, face to flushed, sweaty face.

Guinan couldn't believe it.

Picard had come back for her. And despite the apparent impossibility of the task, he had plucked her from right under Steej's nose.

"Are you all right?" he asked.

"Fine," Guinan told him, though she thought her heart was going to pound its way out of her chest.

"I'm glad to hear it," the captain said.

"But I must admit," she said, "when I saw you take off into that crowd, I wondered if I was ever going to see you again."

"I only ran," he told her, "so I could have a chance to free you later on."

Guinan could hear the unmistakable sincerity in his voice. It made her ashamed of herself for doubting him.

"But you jeopardized your mission," she told him.

"And I would do it again," Picard assured her.

Unbelievable, she thought. She was starting to get a lump in her throat.

"The question," she said, before it could get any

worse, "is what took you so long? I was in that cell for almost an hour."

Picard chuckled. "I was just waiting for the right moment—the way *you* would have."

For the first time since she left the Nexus, Guinan broke out in a smile.

But then, she had a reason, didn't she? Her faith in her companion had been restored. Once again, he was the wise and courageous man who had risked everything for her.

And not just once, but twice.

Dropping out of the hatch at the end of the access tube, Enabran Tain joined Karrid and Beylen.

Fortunately, there was no one else around to witness their exit, just as there had been no one around to witness their entrance. However, the glinn told himself, that was the *only* sense in which they had been fortunate.

"Let's get out of here," he snarled.

As they made their way toward the nearest airlock, which joined the Chezzulid vessel with an unoccupied Droonan scout ship, Tain went over what had happened in his mind.

Despite everything, the human had betrayed him. It was clear now that he had never intended to allow Tain to get his hands on the female. He had planned this outcome from the beginning.

Could the Cardassian have foreseen such a betrayal? Could he have prevented it? *Of course.* And without question, he should have.

But he had been too eager to get his hands on Picard's

companion and then on Demmix, and he had allowed that eagerness to blind him. And now he had nothing to show for his efforts but a cut above his eye and a frost-damaged hide.

Had he and his men not evacuated the tube so quickly, it might have gone even worse for them. At least they had escaped with their lives.

As always, Tain kept his curses to himself. However, his face burned with shame for the way he had been out-maneuvered.

He wasn't used to it, especially at the hands of a mere alien. On one hand, he had to confess a certain admiration for Picard's talent in the area of duplicity.

On the other, he felt an insatiable thirst for revenge.

Chapter Sixteen

NIKOLAS TOOK A DEEP BREATH and let it out very, very slowly. "That's when he told me he didn't want me back until I was ready to concentrate on my work."

Obal frowned from his seat across the dining table. "That doesn't sound good," he said over the murmur of voices in the mess hall. "Lieutenant Simenon has the captain's ear."

"Oh," said Nikolas, "I have no doubt that Captain Picard will come looking for me the moment he comes back. And not just because of Lieutenant Simenon. Lieutenant Vigo is looking at me funny now. I figure he's the next one to rake me over the coals."

Obal looked concerned. "Perhaps you should consider speaking with Doctor Greyhorse. I'm sure you're not the first crewman who has had trouble falling asleep."

Nikolas shook his head. "Sleep isn't the problem,

Obal. Not really. What I'm in need of, Greyhorse can't prescribe."

The Binderian fell silent, an expression of acute disappointment on his small, pink face.

Inwardly, the ensign cursed himself. All Obal was trying to do was give his friend a little hope, and Nikolas was resisting it at every turn.

But what he had said was true. Greyhorse couldn't help him. As far as he could tell, no one could.

"Listen," he told Obal, "I know you want to give me a hand, and I appreciate it—I really do. But trust me when I tell you that you're wasting your time. There's no cure for what I've got. There's no treatment."

"You can't allow yourself to think that way," the Binderian insisted. "You've got to be positive in your attitude."

Nikolas smiled bitterly. "I'm positive, all right. I'm positive that I'm a drag on you and everyone else on this ship."

"No," said Obal. "That's not you speaking. That's someone else. If you want to pull yourself out of this, you can do it—I know you can."

The ensign was about to disagree when he realized there was someone standing behind him. And in the next heartbeat, the angle of Obal's gaze confirmed it.

What's more, Nikolas had an idea who it was. But, tired and foggy as he was, he would be damned if he would let Hanta get the drop on him.

"Hey, Ensign," said the Bolian, finally making his presence known, "I want to—"

Nikolas didn't give him a chance to finish. Instead, he

pushed himself out from the table as hard as he could, making Hanta cry out with pain and surprise.

Then he got to his feet and drove his fist into the center of Hanta's face, feeling something crack in the process.

The Bolian didn't try to return the favor. He wasn't in any position to do that. All he could do was stagger for a moment and collapse.

But he didn't lose consciousness. Nikolas was glad of that. It gave him a chance to stand over Hanta and gloat.

"What happened?" he asked. "I thought you were going to paint a bulkhead with my guts."

"You idiot," the Bolian rasped, holding the sides of his broken, bloodied nose between his fingertips. "I didn't come here to fight you. I came to *apologize.*"

Nikolas stared at him. "What...?"

"It was getting out of hand," Hanta said. "I wanted to put an end to it." His eyes sparked with animosity. "You're an animal, you know that? You don't belong on a starship."

Nikolas swallowed. The words cut, and cut deeply—mostly because he didn't doubt that Hanta was right.

He didn't belong there anymore. And the sooner he accepted the fact, the better off everyone would be.

Tain hated the idea of meandering through Oblivion without any real destination.

Unfortunately, he had no choice in the matter. He had exhausted all the Zartani hotels and eating places he could find, and come away without any idea of Demmix's whereabouts.

Most frustrating.

His only hope now of finding Picard and his companion was to patrol hull after hull, keeping an eye out for them—and in that regard, his eyes were just as valuable as anyone else's.

As the glinn made his way through the crowd in Six Corners Plaza, where the bomb had gone off just a day earlier, he noted how quickly the site was returning to normal. The debris had been cleared away, the place was full of people, and a few of the vendors were already back in business.

He wished his own enterprise could have gone half as swiftly. He was beginning to loathe Oblivion.

Just then, the Cardassian felt the vibration of his communications device. Taking it out, he said, "Tain here."

"Glinn, this is Jaiman."

Tain turned away from the flood of foot traffic. "What is it?"

"We've tracked down the so-called Cataxxans."

The glinn's heart was filled with a fiery jubilation. "Where are they?" he demanded.

"At a hotel called the Emperor's Eye. It's on the same line as the Sillerac cruiser."

Tain knew the place. "Stay with them. I'll join you as soon as I can."

"As you wish," said Jaiman.

Tain felt a measure of satisfaction as he turned and headed back the other way through the crowd. He didn't care who he had to push out of his way to get by, or how many curses they might hurl at him.

They didn't matter. *Nothing* mattered except the

prospect of finding the Zartani and snatching him out of Picard's hands.

He had been relentless in his pursuit of Demmix, and now Demmix would finally be his—along with Demmix's would-be savior. The human had deceived Tain, made him look foolish. But it was the Cardassian who would have the last laugh.

Anger churning in his belly, Tain picked up the pace as he plowed through the last of the crowd. After all, he wanted to be there when Picard realized he had been undone—and by whom.

The Emperor's Eye was a massive, dome-shaped hotel fashioned from the remains of an opulent, old Denobulan pleasure cruiser.

Picard didn't see a single Zartani in the large, tastefully decorated lobby, with its soaring observation ports at either end, because the Emperor's Eye didn't cater to that clientele. Nonetheless, the captain had reason to believe that Demmix was staying there.

Guinan looked around. "It wouldn't be easy for Demmix to sleep in this place."

"True," said Picard. "But he could do it if he wished. It would just mean waking up at night according to a preset alarm and changing his gas supplement."

"A little risky," his companion noted. "Alarms have been known to fail."

"Demmix's life is in jeopardy either way," the captain pointed out. "The Emperor's Eye would appear to be the lesser evil in that regard."

Guinan nodded. "I suppose."

As they spoke, they stayed as far from the manager's desk as possible. After all, they were fugitives from both the authorities and the Cardassians now, and a conversation with the manager—while potentially illuminating—could too easily get them into trouble.

"Besides," Picard observed, "this is the last hull in this line. If Demmix was headed this way, as the question he posed to the footwear clerk seems to suggest, he could not have had any further destination."

"I think I've found the guest directory," Guinan said. Taking his arm, she turned him in the right direction. "See it?"

"I do," the captain confirmed.

It was a black plastiform workstation with rounded edges and a softly glowing orange screen, stuck away in a remote corner of the lobby. Picard and his companion made their way over there and punched in Demmix's name.

The screen advised them that there was no guest there by that name. The captain wasn't surprised. If Demmix had taken a room there, it would have been under an alias—probably the same one he had used to book passage to Oblivion.

He said as much.

"So what do we do now?" Guinan asked. "Go room to room looking for a Zartani?"

Picard looked around for inspiration—first at the manager's desk, then at the lobby entrance, and finally at one of the big, majestic observation ports.

And suddenly, he had a hunch—the sort that Dixon Hill might have come up with, woefully short of hard data but long on instinct. In Hill's case, his hunches always seemed to work.

The captain hoped he would be as lucky.

"I don't think Demmix is *in* a room," he said. "I think he decided to pursue another option."

"What's that? Sleeping in a hallway?"

It wasn't quite that absurd. "Follow me," said Picard, and led the way back out of the hotel.

Chapter Seventeen

IT WASN'T A SIMPLE MATTER getting access to the Rythrian cargo hauler that Picard had spotted through the observation port of the Emperor's Eye.

He and Guinan had to make their way through a holographic communication center full of flesh-and-blood merchants and their life-sized, ghostly correspondents before they could catch even a glimpse of a likely hatch.

"That should be it," the captain said.

Guinan squinted as she tried to make it out in the soft, projector-lit darkness. "Where? Near that Yridian in the long, purple robe?"

"Actually," Picard said, "he's a hologram."

She frowned. "So he is."

"Look over to the right a little," the captain advised.

Guinan looked. After a moment, she said, "I see it.

But those two bruisers look like they're standing guard over it."

Indeed, there was a Nausicaan standing on either side of the hatch—and Picard had his share of trouble with Nausicaans in the past. But as he was trying to figure out what to do about them, they moved away—obligingly leaving his objective unguarded.

"Lucky break," said Guinan.

"Let's get going," the captain said, "before they decide to come back."

And get going they did. Weaving their way through a maze of figures both solid and ethereal, they reached the hatch and saw it iris open for them.

Their luck really *was* holding. Before either the Nausicaans or anyone else could take any particular interest in what Picard and his companion were doing, they entered the hatch and watched it iris closed again.

The captain found himself in a narrow, worn-looking airlock. And unlike the others he had been in, this one was T-shaped. He had a choice of advancing to the hatch straight ahead of him or entering the one to his left.

"What do you think?" Guinan asked.

Picard recalled the observation port and what it had showed him of the cargo hauler. "I think we go straight ahead."

Like its twin behind them, the hatch irised open, revealing a dimly lit enclosure. Taking out his stolen disruptor, Picard held it in front of him as he led the way inside.

The hold in which he found himself was about half

the size of his ready room back on the *Stargazer*. It was cluttered with squat, dark supply containers, each one branded with a pale blue symbol to show they had been authorized for transport.

However, Picard doubted there was anything in them. The cargo hauler was three decades old if it was a day, and the containers had probably been standing there since the hulk became part of the orbital city.

Certainly, the dust on the floor around them seemed to indicate that. But that wasn't all it indicated.

There were footprints in it—not Picard's or Guinan's, but someone else's. Someone who had been here before them. And at least some of the footprints led to a cluster of containers against the wall.

The captain glanced at his companion, making sure he made eye contact. Then he glanced at the floor. Guinan followed his gaze, saw what there was to see there, then looked up and nodded ever so subtly.

Clearly, there was someone hiding there. Or there had been. If that person was still present, he might be armed—and watching the intruders from his concealment.

Waiting to see what they would do, perhaps. And if they did the wrong thing, it might be answered with a blaze of directed-energy fire.

"Looks empty," Picard said. He looked at his companion. "Let's try the other hatch."

"I'm with you," Guinan said, signaling that she understood what he was up to.

They started back toward the entrance to the place. But before they quite reached it, the captain turned and fired into the suspect cluster of containers, unleashing a beam of pale blue destruction—while Guinan ducked behind the containers arranged near the hatch.

Rolling to his right, the captain looked for return fire. But there wasn't any.

Still, he had a feeling there was someone there. Raising himself up on one knee, he extended his weapon and said, "I know you are there."

There was no answer.

"Come out where I can see you," said the captain, "or I will fire again, and this time I will take my time."

Still no response—at least, at first. Then a shadow separated itself from the other shadows in Picard's sights.

"Now," he said.

The shadow stood up. It was vaguely human-shaped, tall, slender. And as its face was revealed in a shaft of gray light, the captain caught a glimpse of black eyes, bronze skin, and white hair. That could mean only one thing.

It was a Zartani. And not just any Zartani, he realized, but the one he and Guinan had been risking their freedom to find.

"Demmix," he said.

The Zartani looked wary. "Who are *you?*"

The captain smiled. "Not who I appear to be."

Demmix tilted his angular head to the side. "Picard?" he said wonderingly.

"At your service."

Uttering an exclamation of pure joy, the Zartani came out of hiding and embraced him. "I was afraid you had been killed in that explosion in the plaza."

"No such luck," Picard gibed.

Demmix regarded Guinan. "And who's *this?*"

"A friend," Picard assured him. "Without her help, I would never have found you."

The Zartani smiled. "Then I'm glad to see her as well."

The captain made an inclusive gesture. "How did you find this place?"

"I did some research before I left," said Demmix. "As you can see, it came in handy."

"I should tell you," said Picard, "we are not the only ones searching for you. There is a pack of Cardassians on your trail as well."

"Not to mention Steej," Guinan added.

Demmix looked at her, then at the captain. "And who, if I may ask, is Steej?"

The captain tried not to sound too worried. "The director of security in this quadrant of Oblivion."

The Zartani's brow creased. "Why is the director of security looking for *me?*"

Picard sighed. "When the bomb went off in the plaza, I was accused of having set it. Security took me to a detention center, which I escaped with Guinan's assistance. But I was never cleared of the crime. As far as Steej knows, I'm the bomber."

Demmix didn't comment. He just frowned.

"You look concerned," Picard noted.

Demmix snorted. "The man who was supposed to get me off Oblivion is a hunted fugitive. Wouldn't you call that *cause* for concern?"

"Trust me," said the captain. "Now that we are together, we will find a way to reach the *Stargazer.*"

"A way to—?" his friend echoed. He looked stricken. "Don't you have your communicator?"

Picard shook his head. "It was taken from me. Any idea if there's a working com system in this vessel?"

Demmix pointed to another hatch, half-hidden by some containers. "Through there."

"Let's take a look," said the captain.

What they found, at the end of a long corridor, was an open doorway that led to the vessel's control room. It was a bit like the *Stargazer*'s bridge, but a lot smaller.

Fortunately, the rest of the ship wasn't as dusty as the cargo hold. Apparently, the ventilation system was better in some places than in others.

As Picard had hoped, the communications panel looked none the worse for age.

Demmix ran his fingers over its controls. "If we can get this thing going," he said, "we should transmit the information I've gathered on the Ubarrak. That way, if we don't make it to the *Stargazer*, the Federation will still be able to make use of what I've learned."

The captain smiled at him. "Done. But don't worry. We *will* make it back."

The Zartani nodded. "I trust you, Jean-Luc. I always have."

Suddenly, Picard felt a hand on his arm. It was Guinan's—and she didn't look happy.

"What's wrong?" he asked her.

"He's lying," she said.

Picard didn't understand—until her eyes slid in Demmix's direction. The captain turned to the Zartani, who seemed caught between surprise and resentment.

"I beg your pardon?" said Demmix.

"Guinan," Picard said in an appeal for reason, "this man has risked his life to help the Federation. I don't think we should be disparaging him."

Guinan's gaze remained fixed on Demmix. "The information he wants to give us...it's wrong," she said.

"Are you out of your mind?" rasped the Zartani, his voice edged with bitterness.

"Not in the least," Guinan responded. "That data is designed to get the Federation into trouble somehow—maybe when it clashes with the Ubarrak's warships."

Picard put his hand on Demmix's shoulder and said, "You must be mistaken. I *know* Demmix. And I know what the Ubarrak have done to him."

"Nonetheless," Guinan insisted, "he's trying to deceive you. I'm certain of it."

"I don't know who this person is," said the Zartani, "but I didn't come all the way to Oblivion to speak with her." He eyed Picard. "I came to speak with *you.*"

The captain frowned. Demmix was his friend. His first impulse was to trust him. And Starfleet was inclined to trust him as well, or it wouldn't have dispatched one of its officers here to meet him.

But Guinan hadn't been wrong about anything yet. Her instincts were remarkable—better than those of anyone he had ever encountered. If she said Demmix was lying, Picard had to at least entertain the possibility that she was right.

"I don't believe this," said the Zartani, reading

the captain's expression. "You'd take her word before mine?"

Picard sighed. "Please, Demmix. I—"

"I've risked my life to get the Federation this information," the Zartani spat. "My *life*, Jean-Luc! You can't just leave me twisting in the wind!"

The captain was still trying to think of how to respond when he heard a shuffle of feet. He whirled and went for his disruptor pistol.

But he was too late. Tain and a couple of his Cardassians had already entered the room, their own weapons drawn. Tain's lackeys were training their disruptors on Guinan and Demmix.

Only Tain's weapon was trained on Picard.

"It's not that I would mind punching a hole in you," Tain told him ever-so-reasonably, "but it might be easier for everyone if you simply put your stolen property on the floor."

Picard's jaw clenched. He hated the idea of disarming himself. But under the circumstances, he had little choice.

Keeping his disruptor out where the Cardassians could see it, he knelt and slid it across the floor. Then he got up and watched one of Tain's men recover it.

"There, now," said Tain. "Now we can all relax." He turned to the Zartani. "I don't believe you and I have been formally introduced—have we, Demmix?"

The Zartani made a sound of exasperation and turned to Picard. "How could you do this to me, Jean-Luc? I *trusted* you."

Picard chuckled grimly. "Believe me, it was not my intention to bring these people along."

Tain considered Picard. "You know," he said, "you've led me on quite a chase. I admire you for that."

"Thank you," the captain said ironically.

"On the other hand," the Cardassian continued, "it won't stop me from subjecting you to a very long, very painful death. That's the only way I can make certain that others aren't tempted to betray me."

The Cardassian turned to Demmix next. "As for you," he said, "you have something I want. That information you were going to give to the Federation...you'll now be giving to me."

"And if I do?" said Demmix, a tremor in his voice.

Tain laughed. "Not *if*, you fool. *When*. I hope I haven't given you the impression that you and I are haggling here, because we're not. You'll talk, and then I'll have you killed. The only reward you'll get for your cooperation is a quicker death than your friend Picard's."

Demmix blanched.

Tain seemed to take pleasure in the Zartani's discomfort. He turned to Guinan. "And of course, you'll be killed as well."

"Glinn..." said one of the other Cardassians.

"What is it?" Tain asked, his gaze remaining firmly fixed on the captain.

"Before you arrived, as I was eavesdropping in the corridor, I heard the female accuse the Zartani of deception."

Now Tain did spare his underling a glance. "What *kind* of deception are we talking about?"

The underling licked his lips, obviously reluctant to

go on. "She said he was trying to pass off false information, which could get the Federation in trouble—perhaps in the course of a military encounter with the Ubarrak."

Tain looked as if he had been punched in the gut. He glanced at Guinan, then Picard, and finally at Demmix. "I don't like what I'm hearing," he said.

The captain didn't doubt it.

Tain had obviously gone to a great deal of trouble to find Demmix, confident that he would be performing an important service for the Cardassian Union—and perhaps for himself as well, since he would be the one to take credit for it.

Now he had to consider the possibility that he had been led on a wild-goose chase—that all his efforts in Oblivion, all the risks he had taken, had been for naught.

Tain eyed Demmix with cold, dark eyes. "I may have been a bit hasty," said the Cardassian, "when I promised you a quicker death than Picard's."

"Oh?" said Demmix. And to Picard's astonishment, the Zartani smiled, as if he were no longer the least bit concerned about Tain carrying out his threat.

Suddenly, Picard felt a vibration beneath his feet. If he didn't know better, he would have said that the hulk's engine had been activated.

"What's going on?" Tain demanded of Demmix.

"Isn't it obvious?" asked the Zartani.

But his voice was strangely muted. It was then that Picard realized a transparent energy barrier had been erected between Demmix and the rest of them.

Tain scowled. "Whatever it is, *stop* it."

Demmix's smile spread across his face. "Why? So I can earn a quicker death than Picard's?"

As he said it, the captain felt a jolt. It seemed to him that something had collided with their hull.

No, he told himself. *That cannot be right. The city's shields would have deflected any foreign objects.*

Then the truth dawned on him. They hadn't been hit by anything. Their vessel had begun to move, and in the process jerked free of the hulk beside them....

Chapter Eighteen

PICARD SAW TAIN'S LIP CURL as he regarded Demmix. "All right," he said. "Have it your way." And, raising his disruptor, he fired it at the Zartani.

But the beam stalled in midair, fizzling out barely halfway to its intended target. *I was right,* the captain thought. *Demmix has put up a barrier.*

Tain made a sound of derision. "You think a little energy field is going to stop us?"

"Actually," said the Zartani, "I do. But just in case, I've decided to take other measures as well." And he produced a remote-control device, made a show of waggling it about, and replaced it in his jacket.

The Cardassian fired again. But this time his weapon didn't even emit a beam. He looked at it, then frowned at Demmix. "A dampening field."

"That's right," said the Zartani. "So you're not tempted to try damaging this vehicle."

Tain walked up to the barrier and glared through it. "I'll do more than damage your vehicle, Zartani. That's a promise I extend to you."

"What is going on?" Picard asked.

Demmix's smile, as he turned to the captain, became a humorless one. "Haven't you figured it out yet, Jean-Luc? I've been working for the Ubarrak."

Picard didn't understand. "The Ubarrak...?"

"Yes," said the Zartani. "I was doing exactly what your friend Guinan just accused me of—passing bad tactical information to the Federation, information that would give your people a false sense of security. But when the Ubarrak launched a major offensive and your ships reacted to it, you would see that your confidence was built on shifting sand instead of bedrock."

"Because our ace in the hole," said Picard, "wasn't an ace after all."

"And by the time you realized the truth," Demmix continued, "it would be too late. The Ubarrak would have crushed you." He turned to Tain. "Then they could give the Cardassians their undivided attention."

Picard frowned. "But why, Nuadra? The Ubarrak killed your wife, your daughters..."

The Zartani's eyes blazed with anger. "Do you think I need to be reminded of that? My grief for them was so great that I nearly perished. And even after I recovered, I mourned them. I labored under the burden of their loss for five long, black years.

"But I couldn't bring them back. No one could. And I

began to ask myself if I hadn't earned some good in my life, some small recompense for the sadness I had borne."

For the first time, Picard saw the change in his old friend. He wasn't the man the captain had known on Elyrion III—not any longer. He was a threat, just like Tain, and Picard had to treat him as such.

Tain spat in disgust. "A traitor. I wish that bomb had been a bit more lethal."

Demmix's eyes narrowed. "It was you who set it off... wasn't it? You and your underlings?"

"Yes," said the Cardassian, obviously letting his frustration get the better of him.

Picard was beginning to get the picture. "After the bombing of the plaza," he told Demmix, "you still wished to pass on your treacherous information. But you didn't want to risk getting caught by whoever was responsible for it. So you laid down a trail you knew I could follow."

"Yes," said Demmix. "And you did an admirable job of following it." He glanced at Guinan. "With the help of your suspicious friend here."

It made sense. It all made sense. And Picard cursed himself for falling for it.

"Now," Demmix told him, "you and I are going to have a rendezvous after all. But it's going to be with an Ubarrak vessel that's been waiting ten kilometers from here."

The captain understood. "And that's where you'll claim your reward. Tell me... what are the Ubarrak paying these days for a Starfleet captain?"

Demmix chuckled. "We'll soon find out." His eyes slid in Tain's direction. "And the price will be that much higher when the Ubarrak see I've corralled a knowledgeable Cardassian for them as well."

Picard wanted desperately to stop the Zartani. But with the barrier separating them, there was nothing he could do. And even if they never exceeded impulse velocity, they might reach the Ubarrak ship in a matter of minutes.

Suddenly, Guinan—who had been all but forgotten in the exchange—grabbed a disruptor from the nearest Cardassian. Before either he or his comrades could react, she stuck the weapon in one of the room's air vents.

And depressed the trigger.

Picard had just enough time to wonder if Demmix's dampening field extended into the vent. Then he got his answer as the aperture pulsed with a wild, blue light, the disruptor beam wreaking havoc with the conduit beyond and eliciting a backwash of dense, black smoke.

It roiled through the captives' portion of the compartment like a hellish surf, mixing with their air and making it impossible to draw a clean breath. They all started to choke—Guinan, Picard, and the Cardassians as well.

"Damn you," Tain rasped, as he wrestled Guinan for the disruptor, "what have you done?"

Picard knew *exactly* what she had done.

She had put everyone on her side of the barrier in a position to asphyxiate. But if Demmix wanted to, he could save them from that less-than-pleasant fate—simply by lowering the forcefield for a second or two.

Then some of the smoke could escape, and clean air could take its place. It would be enough for his captives to survive. And letting in the smoke wouldn't be a problem for the Zartani, who was a carbon-dioxide breather anyway.

The captain turned to Demmix, who was still visible through the billowing fumes. He could see the panic in the traitor's expression, the indecision. Clearly, Demmix had begun to see what Picard had seen.

But if he was going to drop the barrier, he had to move quickly. Otherwise, his meal tickets would be dead and he would be left without anything to give the Ubarrak.

Part of the captain wanted to drag Tain off Guinan and teach him the finer points of gallantry. But his more prudent part knew he had to be ready if Demmix dropped the barrier, because he wouldn't get a second chance.

However, the Zartani was still hesitating, still weighing his options. For a moment, it looked as though he wasn't going to deactivate the forcefield after all.

Then, as if on impulse, Demmix took out his remote-control device and pressed a stud—probably the one that had activated the field in the first place. Instantly, the lion's share of the smoke was sucked out of the captives' area.

Picard didn't wait to see the Zartani press the stud a second time. Instead, he took an aggressive step forward and launched himself through the smoke-filled air.

Intent on his remote-control device, Demmix didn't seem to see the human coming. Picard plowed into him and bore him to the deck, the device clattering free in the process.

Unfortunately, as fragile as the Zartani could be in certain ways, they were also quite strong. No sooner had Demmix landed on his back than he grabbed Picard by his jacket and sent him flying into the bulkhead behind them.

The captain protected himself from the impact with his forearm, but was jarred when he dropped to the floor. By the time he regrouped, Demmix was coming at him with a vengeance.

And Picard could see that the barrier had closed again. He was the only captive who had made it through.

Rolling to his right, he was able to avoid Demmix's headlong rush. However, they were trapped in a relatively small space. The captain wasn't confident that he could elude the Zartani much longer.

Fortunately, Picard had another option. But to exercise it, he would have to find Demmix's remote-control device among the floating tendrils of smoke he had brought in with him.

Again the Zartani charged him. This time, Picard threw himself to his left—and only narrowly missed being pinned to the bulkhead.

Scrambling to his feet, he took a moment to scan the floor for Demmix's device. *It must be here somewhere,* he told himself. *All I need to do is—*

Then he saw it. It was on the other side of the room, barely visible between trails of smoke.

Demmix was closer to the device, but he seemed neither to have spotted it nor to care. His efforts were focused solely on getting hold of the captain.

And to that end, he had changed his tactics. He was advancing slowly now rather than rushing his attack, trying to back Picard into a corner.

It made the captain's job more difficult. But not insurmountable, he added silently.

"Come," said Demmix, "you know I'm every bit as

quick as you are, and a good deal stronger as well. There's only one way this can end."

"Is that so?" said Picard.

"Don't you think so?"

"Even if I did," the captain said, "what would you have me do? Just surrender to you?"

"It would certainly make it easier on both of us," said Demmix. "And I might be convinced to release you before I turn the others over to the Ubarrak."

"Spare me," Picard told him. "I made a mistake by trusting you once, old friend. Do you really think I would do it again?"

He had barely finished his reply when Demmix came hurtling at him, his hands reaching for the captain's legs. But Picard was ready for him.

Springing into the air, the captain vaulted over his adversary like a little boy playing leapfrog. Then he took two steps, dove in the direction of the remote-control device, and snatched it up as he slid into the bulkhead.

Turning it over in his hands, he found the stud that controlled the energy barrier and depressed it—just before Demmix came crashing into him.

Picard tried to keep the device away from the Zartani, but Demmix was too strong for him. The captain delivered a short, quick blow to his adversary's nose, hoping to damage his gas-supplement, but Demmix just hit him back twice as hard.

Stunned for a moment and unable to see, Picard felt the Zartani try to drag the device from his fingers. But the human held on nonetheless, refusing to relinquish the thing.

Suddenly, Picard couldn't feel Demmix fighting him any longer. He heard a couple of thuds in quick succession, and as his vision cleared, he turned around and saw that the Zartani was lying stretched out on the deck—at the feet of Tain and one of his Cardassians.

The other Cardassian was standing at the vessel's control console. As Picard watched, he looked back at Tain and said, "Done, Glinn."

Tain then took his disruptor—which he had apparently succeeded in recovering from Guinan—trained it on an open section of bulkhead, and fired.

His beam hit the bulkhead with devastating results. Obviously, the dampening field had been lifted.

"There," said Tain. "That's a little more like it."

Guinan moved to Picard's side. "Nice work," she said.

"You too," he replied.

But they were still on course to rendezvous with the Ubarrak. He had to do something about that.

Moving to the end of the console where the helm controls were located, Picard went to work. But he had barely gotten under way when Tain barked at him.

"What are you doing?" the Cardassian demanded, pointing his disruptor at the captain.

"I'm putting us on a course back to Oblivion," Picard explained. "Unless you have an irresistible urge to see the inside of an Ubarrak warship."

"I don't," Tain conceded. "But then, I don't have any particular desire to return to Oblivion either."

"What are you saying?" the captain asked, though he was afraid he knew.

"We're in a warp-cabable ship," said the Cardassian.

"Why not shoot for a more challenging destination? Suddenly, I'm homesick for Cardassia Prime."

"And why would you want to go there?" the captain asked.

"My superiors sent me to Oblivion to get information," said Tain. "As a starship captain, you must be full of information. Now step away from that panel and give me that remote-control device."

Picard frowned. He wasn't looking forward to the prospect of being interrogated on Cardassia Prime.

"And if I don't?" he asked, trying to buy himself time to devise a countermaneuver.

The Cardassian smiled. "If you're not concerned about your own health, think about your friend's." And he swung his weapon over until it was pointed at Guinan.

"Don't worry about me," she said bravely.

But the captain *was* worried about her. Grudgingly, he handed Tain the device.

The Cardassian took a moment to examine it. Then he dropped it on the floor and fired his disruptor, incinerating the device.

"All right," he told his underling at the control console. "Bring us about, Karrid."

A moment later, the captain felt a subtle change in the vessel's thrust. The cargo hauler was turning, adopting a new heading.

"Well done," Tain told the Cardassian called Karrid, who was standing with his back to his superior.

Then, without warning, Tain pointed his weapon at the fellow and squeezed its trigger. The beam struck the Cardassian square in the back and thrust him over the console.

Tain's other henchman whirled to face his superior, no doubt wondering what his comrade had done to arouse Tain's wrath. But instead of telling him, Tain fired again and sent a second body flying across the room.

As the nauseating stench of burned flesh filled the air, Picard saw Tain survey his handiwork. He looked as if he had done nothing more offensive than move a couple of furnishings in his quarters.

"Why did you do that?" Picard asked.

"When things don't go as smoothly as you've planned," said Tain, "it isn't a good idea to leave witnesses to the fact."

Then, with the same casual demeanor, he turned his disruptor pistol on Guinan.

"No!" Picard cried out, instinctively interposing himself between the Cardassian and his companion.

Chapter Nineteen

"HOW TYPICALLY HUMAN," said Tain, as he watched Picard take hold of the female, refusing to let the Cardassian kill her.

Of course, Tain had no intention of killing her.

He felt nothing but disdain for the two of them as he reset the intensity gauge on his weapon. Though he had to keep them alive, he couldn't afford to let them remain conscious all the way from there to Cardassia Prime.

Abruptly, Guinan spoke up. "You pride yourself on being cold-blooded, don't you? But you're not the hard, unforgiving soul you try to be."

Done resetting the guage, Tain laughed at her. "You don't have the slightest idea of what you're talking about."

"Don't I?" asked Guinan. "Outwardly, you frown on

the idea of showing compassion. But deep down, you're as compassionate as anyone. You just don't want to admit it—even to yourself."

Tain regarded her. Clearly, she was trying to distract him—to buy time. But for what purpose?

He scanned the room, trying to find some evidence of what she was up to. Then he realized that they were standing by one of the vessel's ancillary control panels.

He motioned with his disruptor for them to move to the side. "Now!" he barked.

They moved, however reluctantly, and exposed the small, black panel to Tain's scrutiny. He eyed one monitor after the other, assuring himself that nothing had been altered.

Until he got to the screen that kept track of the vehicle's navigational shields. They were down—deactivated. And Tain knew what that meant.

With a cry of rage, he tried to resurrect the shields. But it was too late. Picard and Guinan were already dematerializing, their forms being consumed by pillars of faintly shimmering light.

And so was Demmix's.

Carried on a wave of rage, Tain fired at the human and his companion. But his beams of destructive force went right through them, striking the bulkhead instead. And a moment later, they and the columns of light were all gone.

And Tain was all alone.

One moment, Picard was in the control room of the Rythrian cargo hauler, facing an enraged Tain. The next, he was in one of the *Stargazer's* transporter rooms, gazing at the grateful countenance of his first officer.

And he wasn't alone. Guinan was standing on the pad alongside him. And Demmix was sprawled on the other side of him, still unconscious.

"Good to see you," Ben Zoma said curtly, as he gestured for Greyhorse and a medical team to attend to Demmix.

But the first officer's expression was one of surprise and dismay. It was understandable, given the captain's gaudy color and lack of hair.

"Same here," said Picard, resolving to save the explanation for later. He stepped down off the transporter platform.

"Is Demmix all right?" asked the first officer.

By then, Greyhorse had made a preliminary evaluation. "He'll be fine," said the doctor. Like Ben Zoma, he seemed inclined to ignore the captain's appearance for the moment. "Just a concussion and a few bruises. I'll take him to sickbay."

"You do that," said Picard. "But he'll be under a security watch. And when you are finished with him, I want him in the brig."

Greyhorse looked at him. "I beg your pardon? Isn't he your friend?"

"The brig," the captain repeated. Then he used the ship's intercom to contact Joseph and let him know.

"Whatever you say," Greyhorse muttered. Then he directed his team to place Demmix on an antigrav gurney.

Picard turned to Guinan, who was still standing on

the platform. Holding his hand out to her, he brought her down beside him.

"This is Guinan," he told Ben Zoma. "Without her help, I would be quite dead now."

The first officer inclined his head. "Pleased to meet you."

"Likewise," said Guinan.

Picard addressed Ben Zoma. "I was hoping you had tracked our progress when we broke off from the rest of Oblivion."

"We did," the first officer confirmed. "Hard not to notice when a piece of a city goes flying off on its own."

"Any trouble picking up our biosigns?"

"None. The only problem was deciding how to retrieve you. We couldn't get a transporter lock as long as the vessel's shields were up. And we didn't dare try using a tractor beam. It might have pulled that thing apart."

"Then you saw our shields go down," Picard suggested.

"At which point, we knew you might not have much time. So we got you and Demmix out of there as quickly as possible." Ben Zoma indicated Guinan with a lift of his chin. "And your friend here as well. After all, you had your arm around her. We figured you might want her along for the ride."

Picard smiled at Guinan. "Your intuition was impeccable, Number One."

Abruptly, Wu's voice came to them over the intercom. "Wu to Transporter Room One. That Ubarrak warship is coming after us. One hundred thousand meters and closing."

Picard swore under his breath. The Ubarrak...! They were still coming after Demmix. But he wasn't going to let the Zartani go without a fight.

"Battle stations," said Ben Zoma, without waiting for the captain's authorization. He looked at his friend. "This would be a good time to put Demmix's strategic tech data to work."

Picard sighed. "Unfortunately, Number One—"

"Don't tell me," said Ben Zoma. He glanced at the medical team that was carting the Zartani out of the room. "Demmix didn't have the information he said he did."

The captain clapped his first officer on the shoulder. "We'll have to face the Ubarrak without it."

Ben Zoma managed a smile, if a tense one. "That's all right. You know how much I like a challenge."

Turning Guinan over to the transporter operator for the moment, Picard led the way to the bridge. When he and Ben Zoma got there, Wu was sitting in the center seat and there was an Ubarrak warship fixed on the forward viewscreen.

Wu arched an eyebrow as she caught sight of the captain. But like her colleagues, she refrained from remarking on his appearance.

Relinquishing her chair to Picard, she said, "Weapons range in ten seconds."

"Hail the Ubarrak," Picard said as he sat down.

"No response," Paxton reported from the com station.

"Then send them a message," said the captain. "Tell them the game is over, and they have lost. But if they want to fight us anyway, we will be happy to oblige."

The Ubarrak kept coming—undaunted, it seemed.

"Phasers and torpedoes," said Picard, "full spread, on my mark." He raised his hand. "N—"

But before he could get the word out, he saw the Ubarrak ship veer off and excecute a long, powerful loop. Then she went back the way she came, without taking a single swipe at the *Stargazer.*

Like a dog denied a juicy bone, the captain thought. He smiled to himself.

He would keep his people at battle stations until he was certain that the Ubarrak were gone. But it seemed that they had dodged a very large and deadly bullet.

Dixon Hill would have been proud of them.

Chapter Twenty

PICARD CONSIDERED his old friend through the energy barrier that contained him in his cell. "Demmix," he said, by way of a greeting.

The Zartani said nothing in return. But then, what *could* he say? What could he impart to the captain that would even begin to repair the rift Demmix had created between them?

Picard looked past the prisoner at the bed with which he had been provided. "I apologize for the quality of the accommodations," he said. "We would have preferred to offer you one of our guest quarters. However, you betrayed my trust and tried to use me as a pawn against my own people. Those who do that hardly ever end up in our guest quarters."

Demmix frowned. "What are you going to do with me?"

"I've been giving that some thought," said Picard. "My first officer suggested I throw you out an airlock."

The Zartani's brow creased. "You wouldn't."

"But instead," the captain continued, "I think I'll drop you off on some neutral planet—one that is not too far from Zarta, so you can find your way home."

Demmix didn't seem to like that option either. "Why not take me back to the Federation for judgment? After all, I tried to kidnap one of her captains."

"So you did," Picard agreed. "And as the captain in question, I wouldn't mind that. But the Federation has no jurisdiction over what happens in a place like Oblivion. And with tensions already running high in this sector, the last thing we want is a political incident."

Demmix's features knotted with something very much akin to fear. "But the Ubarrak—"

"Will find you," the captain interjected, "and perhaps extract a price for your failure. It's certainly possible. Then again, maybe you'll be lucky." He smiled. "Who knows?"

"Jean-Luc," said Demmix, "we were friends once. Surely that still means something."

Picard nodded. "It certainly does. It means I'll be up late the next few nights, trying to figure out how I could have misjudged you so badly."

And with that, he left the brig.

Enabran Tain sat with his back against a bulkhead and considered the company he was forced to keep—a couple of staring, openmouthed corpses, both of them the direct result of his own ruthless ambition.

He didn't relish the prospect of spending his entire trip back to Cardassia Prime with such silent and accusing company—and a long trip it would be, considering the limited capabilities of his vehicle's antiquated engines.

Nor did he dare return to Oblivion. Steej and his people would be inclined to ask some rather uncomfortable questions of him.

And then there were the Ubarrak. Their warship hadn't thought enough of him to pry him loose from the cargo hauler, but they couldn't be happy that their plans had been ruined.

Tain sighed.

If he could fix the cargo hauler's communications system—one of the few systems on the ship that no longer worked—he might be able to cut his time in it to a few weeks. Otherwise, it would be months before he reached the nearest Cardassian-controlled star system.

A damned eternity.

In any case, Tain mused, a slow passage might work to his advantage. After all, he had suffered a crashing defeat at a critical juncture in his young career—a defeat at the hands of a mere human, no less—and he would need some time to figure out how to make it sound like a victory.

This time, Paris didn't just show up at Jiterica's quarters. He called ahead to let her know he was coming.

He only waited for a few seconds. Then the doors slid open and he saw Jiterica standing there. She was wearing her containment suit, as he had expected.

Her features were placid, accepting. And maybe a little curious. "You wanted to see me?"

"Mind if I come in?" Paris asked.

"No. Not at all," she said, and stood aside so he could walk past her.

Her quarters looked as they had the first time he saw them—sparsely furnished, but otherwise not unusual. There wasn't any mist in them, dazzling his senses, making him feel things he hadn't wished to feel.

"Do you wish to sit down?" Jiterica asked.

"Thanks," he said, "I'll stand." That way, she didn't have to maneuver herself into a chair.

"All right," she said.

Paris licked his lips. He had practiced what he was going to say, so there wouldn't be any misunderstandings.

"The other day," he began, "when I was here in your quarters...I rushed out because I thought I had violated your privacy. And maybe even more than that."

"I understand," she said. "But there was no violation. I thought I communicated as much."

Paris smiled. "You did."

His reply only seemed to confuse her. "Then why are you speaking of it again?"

This wasn't going to be easy, he told himself. "Because I want to say...what I mean is..."

"Yes?" she said.

Paris could think of only one way to say it. "Before I left your quarters, when I was standing in your midst...I felt something. Something *good*."

Jiterica gazed at him, expressionless. It was impossible to tell how she had taken his remark.

Nonetheless, Paris plunged on. "If it's all right with you, I wouldn't mind feeling it again."

For a time, she just stood there, appearing to absorb what he had told her. The ensign began to wonder if he had overstepped his bounds after all.

Then, just as he was about to tell her to forget he'd said anything, he saw a grin spread across her ghostly face. "I would not mind it, either," she told him.

Paris let out a breath he didn't know he had been holding. It was the best thing she could have said. He wanted to embrace her and share his happiness with her.

But it wasn't possible. The only thing he could embrace was Jiterica's containment suit, and Paris didn't find that option especially appealing.

This wasn't going to be easy, he told himself. Still, he wanted to try to make it work. And as he looked into her eyes, pale and insubstantial as they were, he had a feeling that he wouldn't regret this.

Any of it.

Nikolas sat on the edge of his bed and shook his head.

To take another shot at a fellow crewman, even if he thought it was in self-defense...it was about as stupid a thing as he had ever done. Even more stupid than fighting with Hanta in the first place. And Nikolas couldn't guarantee that he wouldn't do something just as stupid tomorrow.

Or the next day.

Neither could Ben Zoma. That was why he had relieved the ensign of duty pending an investigation of the incident with Hanta in the mess hall.

Nikolas didn't disagree with the first officer's decision. If he were in command of the ship, he would have done exactly the same thing.

Even when he wasn't fighting, he was walking around like a zombie and shirking his responsibilities. He was useless. And he didn't see the situation changing anytime soon.

Not when he couldn't make himself forget Gerda Idun. Not when there were two living reminders of her sitting on the bridge, torturing him with their very presence.

Sometimes Nikolas would see them glaring at him, and realize that he had been staring. He didn't even know for how long. He just knew they didn't like it.

He couldn't blame them, either. It wasn't their fault that they looked and sounded and walked the same way Gerda Idun did, or that she had left while they remained.

Once, Nikolas wouldn't have believed himself capable of such feelings. Other guys fell head-over-heels in love, not him. He had always been too wild, too fickle to let himself get sucked into something like that.

Until now.

He cursed under his breath. He couldn't go on this way. He needed to *do* something before he went nuts altogether.

And it seemed to Nikolas there was only one thing he *could* do.

As Picard entered the lounge, he saw Guinan and Ben Zoma standing by an observation port and chatting. And from the look of it, she was feeling anything but uncomfortable in the first officer's company.

"Sorry," Picard said as he approached them, "but I had some ship's business to take care of. I trust Commander Ben Zoma has been a good host?"

Guinan nodded. "The best. I feel right at home."

Picard smiled. But then, the woman looked so different from the last time he had seen her.

First off, she wasn't purple anymore. Like Picard, she had been restored to her original appearance by Doctor Greyhorse.

For another thing, Guinan's garb was different. Though she had donned a dress similar to the one she had worn in Oblivion, it wasn't the same washed-out shade of gray. It was a vibrant cornflower blue—just like her hat, which was even more extravagant than the one she was wearing when he met her.

However, those weren't the only alterations that Guinan had undergone. It seemed to the captain that her demeanor had changed as well.

She seemed more animated, more optimistic than when he first saw her in that bar back on Oblivion. He wasn't certain why that should be, exactly, but it pleased him.

"So," said Ben Zoma, "if I understand correctly, it was Guinan who distracted the Cardassian in the cargo hauler while you dropped the shields?"

Picard shook his head. "I dropped the shields when the Cardassian killed his henchmen."

"But," said Guinan, "I knew it would take a few moments for you to realize the shields were down and beam us out. So I kept him busy."

"With a little character analysis," the captain added.

He smiled at Guinan. "And no Starfleet counselor could have done a better job of it."

"Where did you learn to do that?" Ben Zoma asked.

Guinan shrugged. "Here and there."

Picard's smile deepened. There was a lot more to Guinan than met the eye. It seemed to him that he could probably spend a lifetime getting to know her and still barely scratch her surface.

She wasn't merely someone who had rescued him from a detention cell. He now thought of Guinan as his friend.

"One thing I don't understand," he told her, "is how you knew Demmix would drop the force barrier between him and us."

"You mean when she fired into the ventilation shaft," Ben Zoma noted.

"Yes," said the captain, "then." But he had barely gotten the confirmation out when the answer came to him. "What am I thinking?" he asked Guinan. "You just *listened.*"

Ben Zoma looked curious. "Listened...?"

"A valuable ability," Picard explained with a wink at his friend, "or so our guest here seems to believe."

"Actually," she said, "there wasn't any *time* to listen. It was just a *hunch.*"

"Really," said the captain.

It occurred to him that Guinan might have learned a bit from him even as he was learning from her. He found the notion a gratifying one indeed.

"You know," said Guinan, in a blatant attempt to change the subject, "I was telling Commander Ben Zoma here that you need to broaden your horizons."

"Really," said Picard. "In what way?"

"Earl Grey?" she said. "At a bar on Oblivion? You could have been more inventive than that."

"What would you recommend?" the captain asked.

"Wait right here," said Guinan.

Then she went over to the replicator slot. When she came back, she was carrying a pair of tall, fluted glasses with a roiling, bloodred liquid inside.

"Here you go," she said, handing a vapor-topped glass to each officer.

"Will I regret this?" asked Ben Zoma.

"Not at all," she assured him.

Picard took a look into his glass. It looked...formidable. Throwing caution to the winds, he took a sip.

And was pleasantly surprised.

"Not bad," he said.

Ben Zoma agreed. "Not bad at all."

"What do you call it?" the captain asked.

"Volcanic Spew." She shrugged. "It's a Tellarite drink."

Ben Zoma turned to his friend. "You know, you ought to hire this woman on as our official bartender."

"I wish I could," Picard said in earnest.

"And while you're at it," his first officer added, "maybe you ought to get yourself a shipboard barber as well. That is, if you're planning on growing your hair back."

"I'm very *much* planning on growing it back," the captain told him sternly. He frowned as he ran his hand over his hairless pate. "This is only a temporary condition, I assure you."

Guinan put a hand over her mouth, badly concealing a smile.

"What?" Picard asked.

"Nothing," she said, her eyes dancing with glee. "Nothing at all."

The captain regarded her. Was it possible that his friend had a knack for foreknowledge she hadn't let on about—and therefore, some sense of how his appearance would evolve in years to come?

No, he told himself firmly. Guinan had many talents, but *no one* could see into the future.

Epilogue

WHEN ULELO EMERGED from the turbolift to begin his shift on the bridge, he was certain that he had made the right decision.

But now that he had been at his post for a couple of hours, he wasn't quite so sure. In fact, he wasn't sure at all.

He hadn't wanted to hurt Emily Bender. That part of the com officer's thinking hadn't changed. After all, she had been good to him. She had been kind beyond all expectation.

But his first duty wasn't to Emily Bender, was it? His first duty was to the ones who had sent him here. Without them, without the mission they had entrusted to him, he would never have boarded the *Stargazer* in the first place.

Ulelo couldn't forget that, or allow anything to distract him from it—not even his friend and the life she had helped him make here. He had to do what he had set out to do. He had to complete his assignment at all costs.

And he would—regardless of what Emily Bender or anyone else might think of him.

With that thought firmly in mind, he scanned the *Stargazer*'s bridge. After all, he had to make certain that no one was looking at him.

Commander Wu, who was sitting in the captain's chair, was going over a supply requisition for the security section while Pierzynski waited patiently at her side. Vigo was bent over his weapons-control panel, running yet another in a series of routine diagnostics. And though it would seem there wasn't much for the helm and navigation officers to do at the moment, the Asmund twins appeared busy as well.

None of them were paying any attention. That made it a good time for him to do what he had to do.

And yet, he hesitated.

Follow your orders, he told himself firmly.

And *still* he hesitated.

Do you want to fail in your mission? the com officer asked himself. *Do you want to fall short of the task that's been assigned to you?*

No, he conceded. He didn't want to fail. He most desperately wanted to carry out the mission assigned to him.

Ulelo thought he had put Emily Bender aside, along with the confusion she sparked in him. However, she had made a deeper impression on him than he had realized.

It was a test of Ulelo's resolve, a test of his devotion to his duty. He couldn't allow himself to come up short.

He had to prove to his comrades that they were right to have given him this mission.

Looking around again, he made sure that he wasn't being observed. Everyone was still going about his or her business, at least for the moment.

Turning his attention to his communications console, Ulelo tapped in a command that would access a seemingly innocent file in his personal database. Then, before he could hesitate again, he tapped in another command and transmitted the entire contents of the file to a distant set of coordinates.

Finally, he used a command code that he had pried from the ship's computer months ago to erase any record of the transmission. That way, he would be free to repeat the procedure after he had put together enough information.

When Ulelo was done, he took stock of the bridge again. No one seemed to have any idea of what he had been up to. Once again, he had been successful in his deception.

But then, he was nothing if not careful. It was, no doubt, one of the reasons he had been given such an important mission.

He just wished he remembered more about the life he led before he was assigned to the *Stargazer.* After all, it could only have helped him to remain faithful to his purpose.

And he wished as well that he could carry out his task without having to conceal it from Emily Bender.

Look for STAR TREK fiction from Pocket Books

Star Trek®

Star Trek®: The Original Series

Star Trek: The Next Generation®

Novelizations

Encounter at Farpoint • David Gerrold
Unification • Jeri Taylor
Relics • Michael Jan Friedman
Descent • Diane Carey
All Good Things... • Michael Jan Friedman
Star Trek: Klingon • Dean Wesley Smith & Kristine Kathryn Rusch
Star Trek Generations • J.M. Dillard
Star Trek: First Contact • J.M. Dillard
Star Trek: Insurrection • J.M. Dillard
Star Trek: Nemesis • J.M. Dillard

#1 • *Ghost Ship* • Diane Carey
#2 • *The Peacekeepers* • Gene DeWeese
#3 • *The Children of Hamlin* • Carmen Carter
#4 • *Survivors* • Jean Lorrah
#5 • *Strike Zone* • Peter David
#6 • *Power Hungry* • Howard Weinstein
#7 • *Masks* • John Vornholt
#8 • *The Captain's Honor* • David & Daniel Dvorkin
#9 • *A Call to Darkness* • Michael Jan Friedman
#10 • *A Rock and a Hard Place* • Peter David
#11 • *Gulliver's Fugitives* • Keith Sharee
#12 • *Doomsday World* • Carter, David, Friedman & Greenberger
#13 • *The Eyes of the Beholders* • A.C. Crispin
#14 • *Exiles* • Howard Weinstein
#15 • *Fortune's Light* • Michael Jan Friedman
#16 • *Contamination* • John Vornholt
#17 • *Boogeymen* • Mel Gilden
#18 • *Q-in-Law* • Peter David
#19 • *Perchance to Dream* • Howard Weinstein
#20 • *Spartacus* • T.L. Mancour
#21 • *Chains of Command* • W.A. McCay & E.L. Flood
#22 • *Imbalance* • V.E. Mitchell
#23 • *War Drums* • John Vornholt
#24 • *Nightshade* • Laurell K. Hamilton
#25 • *Grounded* • David Bischoff
#26 • *The Romulan Prize* • Simon Hawke
#27 • *Guises of the Mind* • Rebecca Neason
#28 • *Here There Be Dragons* • John Peel
#29 • *Sins of Commission* • Susan Wright
#30 • *Debtor's Planet* • W.R. Thompson
#31 • *Foreign Foes* • Dave Galanter & Greg Brodeur
#32 • *Requiem* • Michael Jan Friedman & Kevin Ryan
#33 • *Balance of Power* • Dafydd ab Hugh

Star Trek: Deep Space Nine®

#4 • *Lesser Evil* • Robert Simpson

Rising Son • S.D. Perry

The Left Hand of Destiny, Books One and *Two* • J.G. Hertzler & Jeffrey Lang

Star Trek: Voyager®

Mosaic • Jeri Taylor

Pathways • Jeri Taylor

Captain Proton: Defender of the Earth • D.W. "Prof" Smith

The Nanotech War • Steve Piziks

Novelizations

Caretaker • L.A. Graf

Flashback • Diane Carey

Day of Honor • Michael Jan Friedman

Equinox • Diane Carey

Endgame • Diane Carey & Christie Golden

#1 • *Caretaker* • L.A. Graf

#2 • *The Escape* • Dean Wesley Smith & Kristine Kathryn Rusch

#3 • *Ragnarok* • Nathan Archer

#4 • *Violations* • Susan Wright

#5 • *Incident at Arbuk* • John Gregory Betancourt

#6 • *The Murdered Sun* • Christie Golden

#7 • *Ghost of a Chance* • Mark A. Garland & Charles G. McGraw

#8 • *Cybersong* • S.N. Lewitt

#9 • *Invasion!* #4: *The Final Fury* • Dafydd ab Hugh

#10 • *Bless the Beasts* • Karen Haber

#11 • *The Garden* • Melissa Scott

#12 • *Chrysalis* • David Niall Wilson

#13 • *The Black Shore* • Greg Cox

#14 • *Marooned* • Christie Golden

#15 • *Echoes* • Dean Wesley Smith, Kristine Kathryn Rusch & Nina Kiriki Hoffman

#16 • *Seven of Nine* • Christie Golden

#17 • *Death of a Neutron Star* • Eric Kotani

#18 • *Battle Lines* • Dave Galanter & Greg Brodeur

#19-21 • *Dark Matters* • Christie Golden

#19 • *Cloak and Dagger*

#20 • *Ghost Dance*

#21 • *Shadow of Heaven*

Books set after the series

Homecoming • Christie Golden

The Farther Shore • Christie Golden

Enterprise®

Novelizations

Broken Bow • Diane Carey
Shockwave • Paul Ruditis
By the Book • Dean Wesley Smith & Kristine Kathryn Rusch
What Price Honor • Dave Stern
Surak's Soul • J.M. Dillard

Star Trek®: New Frontier

New Frontier #1-4 Collector's Edition • Peter David
   #1 • *House of Cards*
   #2 • *Into the Void*
   #3 • *The Two-Front War*
   #4 • *End Game*
#5 • *Martyr* • Peter David
#6 • *Fire on High* • Peter David
The Captain's Table #5: *Once Burned* • Peter David
Double Helix #5: *Double or Nothing* • Peter David
#7 • *The Quiet Place* • Peter David
#8 • *Dark Allies* • Peter David
#9-11 • *Excalibur* • Peter David
   #9 • *Requiem*
   #10 • *Renaissance*
   #11 • *Restoration*
Gateways #6: *Cold Wars* • Peter David
Gateways #7: *What Lay Beyond:* "Death After Life" • Peter David
#12 • *Being Human* • Peter David

Star Trek®: Stargazer

The Valiant • Michael Jan Friedman
Double Helix #6: *The First Virtue* • Michael Jan Friedman and Christie
   Golden
Gauntlet • Michael Jan Friedman
Progenitor • Michael Jan Friedman
Three • Michael Jan Friedman
Oblivion • Michael Jan Friedman

Star Trek®: Starfleet Corps of Engineers (eBooks)

Have Tech, Will Travel (paperback) • various
 #1 • *The Belly of the Beast* • Dean Wesley Smith
 #2 • *Fatal Error* • Keith R.A. DeCandido

#4 • *Treaty's Law* • Dean Wesley Smith & Kristine Kathryn Rusch
The Television Episode • Michael Jan Friedman
Day of Honor Omnibus • various

Star Trek®: The Captain's Table

#1 • *War Dragons* • L.A. Graf
#2 • *Dujonian's Hoard* • Michael Jan Friedman
#3 • *The Mist* • Dean Wesley Smith & Kristine Kathryn Rusch
#4 • *Fire Ship* • Diane Carey
#5 • *Once Burned* • Peter David
#6 • *Where Sea Meets Sky* • Jerry Oltion
The Captain's Table Omnibus • various

Star Trek®: The Dominion War

#1 • *Behind Enemy Lines* • John Vornholt
#2 • *Call to Arms...* • Diane Carey
#3 • *Tunnel Through the Stars* • John Vornholt
#4 • *...Sacrifice of Angels* • Diane Carey

Star Trek®: Section 31™

Rogue • Andy Mangels & Michael A. Martin
Shadow • Dean Wesley Smith & Kristine Kathryn Rusch
Cloak • S.D. Perry
Abyss • David Weddle & Jeffrey Lang

Star Trek®: Gateways

#1 • *One Small Step* • Susan Wright
#2 • *Chainmail* • Diane Carey
#3 • *Doors Into Chaos* • Robert Greenberger
#4 • *Demons of Air and Darkness* • Keith R.A. DeCandido
#5 • *No Man's Land* • Christie Golden
#6 • *Cold Wars* • Peter David
#7 • *What Lay Beyond* • various
Epilogue: Here There Be Monsters • Keith R.A. DeCandido

Star Trek® The Lost Era

The Sundered • Michael A. Martin & Andy Mangels
Serpents Among the Ruins • David R. George III

Star Trek® Omnibus Editions

Invasion! Omnibus • various
Day of Honor Omnibus • various

The Captain's Table Omnibus • various
Double Helix Omnibus • various
Star Trek: Odyssey • William Shatner with Judith and Garfield Reeves-Stevens
Millennium Omnibus • Judith and Garfield Reeves-Stevens
Starfleet: Year One • Michael Jan Friedman

Star Trek® Short Story Anthologies

Strange New Worlds, vol. I, II, III, IV, V, and VI • Dean Wesley Smith, ed.
The Lives of Dax • Marco Palmieri, ed.
Enterprise Logs • Carol Greenburg, ed.
The Amazing Stories • various
Prophecy and change • Marco Palmieri, ed.

Other Star Trek® Fiction

Legends of the Ferengi • Ira Steven Behr & Robert Hewitt Wolfe
Adventures in Time and Space • Mary P. Taylor, ed.
Captain Proton: Defender of the Earth • D.W. "Prof" Smith
New Worlds, New Civilizations • Michael Jan Friedman
The Badlands, Books One and *Two* • Susan Wright
The Klingon Hamlet • Wil'yam Shex'pir
Dark Passions, Books One and *Two* • Susan Wright
The Brave and the Bold, Books One and *Two* • Keith R.A. DeCandido

STAR TREK
SECTION 31

BASHIR
Never heard of it.

SLOAN
We keep a low profile....
We search out and identify
potential dangers to the
Federation.

BASHIR
And Starfleet sanctions
what you're doing?

SLOAN
We're an autonomous
department.

BASHIR
Authorized by whom?

SLOAN
Section Thirty-One was
part of the original
Starfleet Charter.

BASHIR
That was two hundred years
ago. Are you telling me
you've been on your own
ever since? Without specific
orders? Accountable to
nobody but yourselves?

SLOAN
You make it sound so
ominous.

BASHIR
Isn't it?

No law. No conscience. No stopping them.
A four book series available wherever books are sold.

Excerpt adapted from Star Trek:Deep Space Nine® "Inquisition"
written by Bradley Thompson & David Weddle.
2161.01